From Susan
Christmas, 2020
We made it ♡

TWISTED VEIL

CHRISTENA ROSE

 FriesenPress

Suite 300 - 990 Fort St
Victoria, BC, V8V 3K2
Canada

www.friesenpress.com

ISBN
978-1-5255-3947-3 (Hardcover)
978-1-5255-3948-0 (Paperback)
978-1-5255-3949-7 (eBook)

1. FICTION, OCCULT & SUPERNATURAL

Distributed to the trade by The Ingram Book Company

PRELUDE TO DESCENT

The raven's song cut through the forest at the hour of sunset. Its harsh cry was a message to a girl. The day she lived for had come at last. She took off running in a flurry of black hair and threadbare cotton. Her petitions were finally answered. She could feel it in the cool soil beneath her feet, she could hear it in the wind that swept through the trees, and she could see it in the moon above the woodland canopy.

The girl moved deftly and leapt noiselessly over each rock and bush. It was *her* forest. She owned every root that gripped the earth and every bird that touched the sky. Nothing would stop her, and *nothing* would dare to get in her way.

Like wildfire, she covered ground until the sound of rushing water slowed her nimble approach. The girl crept into the shadows and hid herself amongst the willow trees. A river flowed at her side. It was a natural division of two very different worlds. One world was that of opportunity and privilege, while the other was that of obscurity and hardship. These two worlds would remain separate, if not for a single bridge that connected them. The girl watched that very bridge in anticipation, for the time had come.

He was home.

An orb of golden light appeared midst the bushes that thrived along the riverside. The girl's lips parted expectantly. She did not blink—she did not even breathe.

A boy holding a lantern stepped out of the darkness and onto the bridge. For the first time in years, the girl experienced a pure, untainted happiness. The blood in her veins warmed her soul and woke her sleeping heart.

The four years he spent away had changed him. The boy looked different. He stood taller with a broad frame and a lean build. He was thinner, which highlighted all the smooth curves and fine features of his face. He had seen the world and experienced things that she would never understand. She feared that he would not remember her, for the *boy* she knew was gone and a *man* stood in his place.

The wooden bridge creaked as the man placed the lantern by his feet. He rested his forearms on the railing, hung his head, and took a few deep, soothing breaths. The girl watched him intently and noticed his shaking hands. He rubbed them together to calm the nervous twitch.

For some reason, his suffering affected her. The girl tilted her head in consideration. There was a pain in her chest that she did not recognize. The sensation pulled her out of the willows. As she tiptoed through the ferns, her foot landed on a fallen branch. It snapped. The sound was enough to give her away, and the young man reacted like a frightened deer. He jumped, turned, and gripped fiercely to the railing behind him. They saw each other and stared, wide-eyed and motionless. His heart raced until he recognized the girl in the shadows. She had changed since he saw her last. She had grown from a child, to a teenage girl.

Although the youngster he remembered was gone, many of her features remained the same. Her pretty face was still hidden behind a veil of tangled hair, her bare feet were still black with filth, and her expression was still made of stone. She was the same feral girl that traipsed through the forest, and watched him from the willows.

"Hello," he called out to her.

"Hello. Are you all right?" The girl pointed at the young man's iron grip.

He looked at his hands and released the wooden railing. "Just a little touchy these days," he answered.

The girl stepped off the bank and joined the young man on the bridge. She closed the space between them. "I missed you." The words left her lips before she could stop them. She had been waiting to speak them for far too long.

The young man was surprised. "You have?"

"Yes," she replied simply.

Taken aback and lost for words, he forced a smile on his wary face. She did not smile. She only asked, "Did you miss me?"

"I missed home," he answered honesty.

The girl's expression stayed the same. Her pursed lips and empty stare revealed nothing. "But you did not miss me." She spoke the words for him. A new pain blossomed inside of her.

The young man's eyes narrowed. "I'm not sure why you would ask."

"Because I've been waiting for you." Her voice was tender. It was the first time he saw the spark of life in her grey eyes.

"Why would you wait for me?" The young man's face was grave. "Do you realize how many times I was close to never coming back?"

She took a step closer and looked directly in his eyes. "I *knew* you would return," she said with absolute certainty. Feeling uncomfortable, the young man took a step back. The girl saw him move away and her gaze fell. She leaned against the railing and whispered, "I waited . . . because I love you. I have always loved you."

The young man was not prepared for the girl's sincere declaration. His heart flooded with sympathy, for there was *no way* he could ever love her back.

In his most gentle voice, he said, "You don't really love me. One day you'll understand. You're still so young."

"But I'm older now." She stepped back so he could look at her. He just stared with apologetic eyes. He pitied her. Why wouldn't he? The girl looked down at her frayed dress and dirty feet.

The young man saw her shame. He hated making her feel that way. "I'm sorry. We're just . . . too different." It was the truth. He could not lie to her. The girl believed in many strange things. She walked a dark path that he could never follow.

"So, you think you're better than me?" Her voice had turned venomous. "Well you're wrong." The girl backed off the bridge. Her anger was palpable as she disappeared between the weeping boughs that skirted the forest.

"No! That's not what I meant," he exclaimed. The young man wanted her to understand, but he could not find the words. He could not tell her how he truly felt; that even after living through four years of hell, even after seeing the world at its worst, the girl still frightened him.

✘ ✘ ✘

A single tear fell from a grey eye. It was removed in one angry swipe. At that moment, a girl's heart froze over, like thick frost on a cool winter morning. All the love and hatred was locked within. She gritted her teeth as the powerful emotions scarred her soul. She fell to her knees and raked her hands through the black soil. The pain writhed and stirred the dark storm that grew inside of her. She could not let him go. One day he would belong to her, she vowed. He would love her, willingly or not.

The girl relinquished her last bit innocence and sealed her fate. She then closed her eyes, threw her head back, and smiled wickedly at the moon.

ASHES TO EMBERS

The day had come—the day that marked the death of a young girl. Change was inevitable, but it was hard to let go, especially of the little girl I knew so well. Like an insect trapped under a bell jar, she had to be set free. In the blink of an eye, she was gone. She vanished and left me staring at a stranger in the mirror. The next chapter had arrived, and the days to follow were written in mystery.

Enlightened and educated at last, I was facing a strange new everything, and it scared me. It was the kind of fear that intoxicated and thrilled you until nothing else mattered. Instead of fighting it, I chose to revel in the haze while wearing metaphorical rose-colored glasses. There was no better option. The unknown, the indefinite, and the uncertain were all there was left. My life was once sketched out and designed, like a custom-fit future of youthful ignorance. But, things change, people change, and so do our expectations.

Out of nowhere, my expectations of the future were shattered into a trillion little pieces. Everyone saw me as a clueless victim. They saw a betrayal. Luckily, my pride cast the shattered pieces in a different light. I saw a gift, not a betrayal, but a gift of liberation. My spirit was cut loose and set free from an existence that was slowly killing me. Not killing me physically, but killing the flame that burned deep inside. The flame that made us all run barefoot through a grassy field, just 'cause—that made us close our eyes while breathing the salty air off the sea—that made us *roll the top down* to reach for the sky while shouting at an empty road. It was a gift, because in the end my flame was just a spark. My flame was just an ember waiting to be rekindled.

It all started the first year of art school. I met someone, and together we fell wilfully into place. At the time, I thought we were the perfect fit—Emilie and her beau, forever hand-in-hand. In reality, we were two naive puzzle pieces, mismatched and stubbornly forced together.

For nearly two years, I was convinced that sharing a creative mind was enough. His incredible talent intrigued me from the beginning. His look was unique and like no other. He was quiet, which I took as mysterious. He separated himself from the others, which I took as individuality. He seemed so different in a special kind of way, but I was mistaken. He was, in fact, self-absorbed with an offbeat style that was just a sad attempt at a social statement.

Hindsight is an amazing thing.

Back when the relationship began, I was a dreamer. I imagined us living together one day in some trendy urban loft. We would look down from our balcony onto a city filled with promise. Galleries would fight to show our artwork, and our admirers would shower us with pretty hors d'oeuvres and pink champagne. Together, we had the ambition and potential to be unstoppable. Regardless, life is relentless and filled with many twists. Sometimes you are forced to alter your hopes and dreams. My view of the future was evolving into something very different. Of course, there was *one thing* that helped change my perspective; I had been replaced.

To be fair, we were never really in love. Not like the love you read about, or watch on some big silver screen, anyway. From the beginning I tried to find a deeper connection with him—I really did. In theory, we made sense, but it was too hard to forget about the past. It was too hard to ignore the realities of life and just let him in. I did not mean to close myself off; I simply knew that nothing was forever. Regardless of how hard you fought for those who mattered, they always left in the end.

Whether it was his fault or mine, the relationship was doomed from the start. When it mattered most, the desire to fight for each other was nonexistent. So quickly, the dreams had faded and we grew apart. There was no electricity between us—there was no magic. Time had changed everything. So when my expectations shattered, I was able to pick up the pieces, throw them away, and move on. I was given a fresh start, like a present wrapped in independence and topped with a giant silver bow. Alone but not lonely, I faced the last day of school—the last day of my old life, and felt free.

Leaving my final class behind, I walked the hallway, running my hand along the white walls. My thoughts were consumed with the infinite possibilities of my untouched future. When my fingertips came to rest on something metallic and cold, the daydream slipped away. It was the frame of a large bulletin board by an exit to the parking lot. I walked those halls twice a day, every day, and never stopped to read what was posted. For once, there was no hurry. I was not late for a lecture or rushing to hand in an assignment. Those stressful days were over, and I finally had nowhere to be.

The board was littered with help-lines and an array of colorful pamphlets. There were flyers about everything and anything, from school funding to summer workshops. Some students were looking to move off campus while others were looking to move in. It was a random patchwork of florescent papers and flashy advertisements.

While standing there alone, I suddenly got the strangest feeling. Almost like someone else was there . . . watching me. My skin tingled when a chill swept across my face and neck. I looked around and saw no one. Then the outside door rattled with the wind, and my heart skipped. A breeze seeped through the cracks and whistled eerily down the empty hall. All the flyers and glossy pamphlets lifted to reveal a job posting hidden beneath. It caught my eye, even though it was small and inconspicuous. I pulled it off the board to get a closer look. It was on expensive floral stationery and handwritten in elegant cursive.

Caretaker Needed

Looking for live-in assistance, 5 days a week, for a Miss Adalynn King. Must be reliable, hardworking, and kind. Location: The Kingsgrove Estate in Willow Vale. Please call the number below to set up an interview.

Willow Vale was in the Deep South, and rather far away. The idea of leaving it all behind to start over was tempting. Besides, I was unemployed and needed the money.

Why not call?

On a whim, I took the paper and stuffed it in my messenger bag.

I turned toward the doorway and looked through the narrow window at the parking lot. A large raven was perched on the hood of my car. It looked odd standing there in dark contrast to the bright white paint. I pushed open the heavy metal door. The sound of it closing behind me spooked the bird and it took flight. I looked up at the overcast sky and watched the raven fly south with its powerful satin wings.

X X X

Although the night was young, with nowhere else to go, I decided to head home. Actually, it was not my home at all; it was just a shabby apartment I once shared with a certain someone. That particular evening, that someone was out with friends—*his* friends, who were once *our* friends.

With a sigh, I navigated through a maze of half-packed boxes and sat at my desk. While staring up at nothing, a reluctant memory came to mind. It was the exact moment our relationship reached its bitter end. In that moment, everything changed . . .

"I'm not sorry, Emilie," he confessed, unable to look me in the eye. "I've found my muse."

My ears rang, as if a shotgun had just went off next to them. I barely heard the ridiculous words coming out of his mouth.

"You should probably leave." He buried his hands deep in his pockets. I stared at the untied laces of his worn Chuck Taylors and stopped listening altogether.

"Having you here is . . . it's too much. I can't focus. It's best that you leave," he insisted. Little did he know, I was already halfway out the door.

Head bowed, I forced the memory out of my mind. It was time to bury the past for good and focus on something better. I rummaged through my bag for the piece of crumpled stationery and flattened it on my lap. Without overthinking, I took a deep breath, picked up the phone, and dialed. An older woman with a southern drawl answered. Her voice sounded like honey, like when it starts to harden and crystallize around the edges. I bet when she was younger it sounded more like fresh, golden nectar—slow and sweet.

I introduced myself. "Hello. My name is Emilie Wyld. I saw your ad posted at my school about the caretaker position?"

"Well, well, isn't this just my day! My name is Jo-Anne Peters. Call me JoJo. I'm Miss King's nurse and dear friend." The woman cleared her throat. "Lately, I've been findin' it hard to help out at Kingsgrove. It's 'cause of my age, you know. I need someone who can stay there and make sure it's taken care of. As for Miss King, she'd be no trouble at all. Ada is very independent and can to do many things on her own. She's sixty years young, I always say."

"If you don't mind me asking, why does Miss King need a caretaker if she is so . . . capable?"

I could hear the clatter of dishware, a teacup placed onto its saucer. "Well, the estate's so big that we can hardly keep up." She chuckled. "Then of course, there's the matter of Adalynn's situation."

"Situation?" My brow furrowed.

"When Adalynn was just a little girl, she had an accident. Poor thing was never the same. Hasn't spoken a single word since that very day. I'm guessin' it was an awful shock to her system." JoJo sipped her beverage before going on. "Ada never did learn how to read or write, or do that sign language stuff neither. It can be difficult to communicate with her at times, but we find a way to get her what she needs." JoJo Peters muffled a cough then asked, "So, Miss Wyld, what makes you think you're up for this job anyhow?"

I answered truthfully. "My experience is limited, but I did live with my grandmother until she passed away. I cooked and cleaned for her. I also did the groceries and cared for the house, especially when she was sick. And now that school is over, I'll need a place to live. That being said, as an artist, I'm always looking for a little inspiration. This job sounds like an interesting new adventure, and I'd love to come help Miss King." I smiled at the phone as if JoJo Peters could see. For some unknown reason, my desire for the job burned deep.

Why did it feel like my heart would break if she turned me down?

There was something mysterious and slightly romantic about the whole thing. I was consumed with curiosity. I *had* to know more about this mute woman tucked away in Willow Vale.

"An artist, you say? Well, Kingsgrove is simply breathtakin'. I'm sure you'd love it. There's a nice lookin' river just a stone's throw away from the estate. And the house! Well . . . the house is positively charming, to say the least."

JoJo went on describing what she expected in regards to the position, such as housecleaning, grounds keeping, and running errands. She spoke in her honey-like voice with unfamiliar terms and phrases. Every inflection was especially polite and sugary sweet. I listened intently and soon realized that JoJo was looking to hire a companion for Miss King, as well as a caretaker. I was asked to read to her, share meals, and simply keep the woman company. It was overwhelming, but the job paid well and offered free room and board. Apparently, the old servant's quarters at Kingsgrove were *just lovely*. On top of that, JoJo would visit every weekend and see to Miss King in a way only a nurse could. During that time, I was free to do as I pleased.

The nurse prattled on, and before I knew it, she was giving me directions to Willow Vale. Apparently, she was eager to fill the position and wanted me to start straight away, which suited me just fine.

It surprised me how easily JoJo made up her mind. Despite my inexperience, she was quite convinced. "I have a good feelin' 'bout you, Emilie. And I have a knack for these sorts of things, you know. My gut is telling me you're the right fit, and my gut rarely leads me astray."

With no time to think it through, I thanked JoJo for the opportunity and promised to arrive sometime on Monday evening. I hung up and raked a hand through my hair while staring down at the receiver. The dial tone hummed glaringly in the empty apartment. It was the sound of me sealing fate with a deadbolt and throwing away the key. It all happened so fast that my stomach was in knots and my head spun with nervous excitement.

✘ ✘ ✘

The next couple days were filled with well wishes and sad farewells. My entire life was spent in or around the city. Leaving it all behind was bittersweet. From the vintage clothing store on Marie Avenue to the cigarette-burned stool at my favorite coffee shop, I would truly miss these nooks and crevices nestled between stoplight and bus stop. On the other hand, my old apartment would not be missed and just as easily forgotten. As much as I tried to avoid it, packing my things was a necessary evil. Thankfully, there was not much that I held near and dear. Only two things were truly special to me: an old beat-up 1977 Trans Am and an antique silver locket. The car belonged to my mother when she was alive, and the locket was given to me by my grandmother. The oval pendent had a flying hawk embossed in the silver. There were no tiny pictures inside. It was empty. I wore it every day and touched the locket constantly as a nervous habit. I liked the way it felt between my fingers.

After stuffing my car with some clothes, an easel, and a trunk full of random bits and art supplies, I decided to leave the rest behind. It was time to go. The strange, new everything beckoned me with its hazy, outstretched hand. It was time to run away from the naive, little girl I once was. There was no looking back. My last *goodbye* was scribbled on the chalkboard in the kitchen, the house key was left on the counter, and the door was closed behind me. With my head held high, I got into my old Trans Am and drove south to Willow Vale, non-stop through the pouring rain and straight on to the unknown.

LONELY CREATURES

The Trans Am flew down the empty highway, turning the outside world into nothing but a sunny blur. The rain had finally stopped and the hot sun beat relentlessly through the windshield. I rolled the windows down and sang off-tune to the music on the radio. Hours passed and the scenery changed rapidly, like a kaleidoscope of small towns and farmland. Eventually, the southbound road took me to the backwoods of Willow Vale. Straight away, I received an evil eye from a few weathered locals. They knew I was an outsider, lost in their sleepy town.

Somewhere on the outskirts of Willow Vale, I found Kings Lane at last. It was a picturesque dirt road that snaked along the forest floor. The sun cast rays of light through a canopy of dense green. I craned my neck to breathe the balmy air and soak in the ambience. It was exactly what I had hoped for—a place where someone could lose themselves completely. It was a place where you came to forget it all.

I started to think that Kings Lane was never-ending just as it turned into to an open grove. In disbelief, I rubbed my eyes and blinked hard. Never had I seen such a place. Kingsgrove was large, and both menacing and lovely. The Victorian-style mansion was impressive, though it had surely seen better days. Every pillar and gable was scaled with chipped paint, while the house itself was snarled in cypress vines and unruly thickets. The estate was a powerful display of untamed beauty. For a moment, I imagined when it was first built. I could almost see a little girl, adorned with ribbons and lace, running along the veranda. It was a picture of the past in a forgotten place, frozen in time. Its magnificence was intimidating.

The house, being as captivating as it was, nearly overshadowed the cemetery beside it. My skin crawled as I stepped out of the car, fully entranced. With the door left open behind me, I walked across the grounds to stop and gawk at the gothic display. A gated trellis made of iron and withered vines guarded the dead. The grass was untrimmed, and the creeping moss climbed the tombstones within. Flourishing in the middle of the cemetery was a large willow tree. Its lush, weeping branches sang the song of many little birds. Unconsciously, I held the locket that hung from my neck. For a while, I just stood there as the world hazed around me until the sound of a clearing throat startled everything back into focus.

I jumped and twisted around to see a petite woman in white. She wore stark white sneakers, a nursing smock, and a 'fro of plush curls.

With a large, toothy grin, the woman clasped her chest. "I'm sorry dear! Didn't mean to startle you. I'm JoJo."

"Hello there. Emilie Wyld." We shook hands. Hers felt both soft and boney in mine.

"Well, aren't you a pretty little thing. Ada will take to you just fine. And my, my! Look at all that blonde hair! It's as bright as a fresh magnolia in spring." She held out a long strand and stared at it. I shyly combed it back with my hand and laughed uncomfortably. JoJo just kept on smiling. "I see you've found Ada's kin." The little woman smiled warmly at the cemetery beyond the gate.

"It was unexpected," I said honestly. Conveniently enough, JoJo forgot to mention a cemetery during my interview.

"Peaceful, isn't it?" A tone of sadness lay just below the surface of her voice. "Adalynn is the last of her family alive and the youngest of five girls, you know," the nurse said and then took me by the arm. She pulled me toward the house, tearing my gaze off the yard of granite stones. "Come, come. Let me introduce you to Miss King. You can explore later. Mustn't be rude now. We've been expectin' you."

Upon entering Kingsgrove, goose bumps trickled up my arms and spilled down my spine. I tried to rub the eerie chills away, but the building was so large and commanding. It seemed to have a pulse—it seemed to have a life of its own. Kingsgrove was a living creature made of timber and stone, and as I entered the mouth of the beast, somewhere deep inside I knew my world would never be the same.

For a moment, I actually thought I was dreaming. The contemporary world was nowhere to be seen! Every wall was covered in lavish paper and trimmed with layers of elaborate moulding. Filling the entryway was a grand staircase, centered with opposing flights leading to the east and west wing. The railings were curled into black locks of iron with matching candelabras atop each bottom post. A large baroque-style mirror hung on the first landing. The silvered glass was fogged and speckled in parts. Everything was out-dated and quite old, yet seemingly luxurious. Although it was sun-stained, chipped, and tarnished, the home transcended time.

As my eyes continued to wander, my mind began to question how long Miss King had lived there alone. A profound sadness came over me at that moment. There was a heavy impression of misery in the dusty air. It was ingrained in the faded walls around me. Adalynn had spent many lonely years trapped in her own mind. The atmosphere was plagued with her isolation. It was such a large home for only one woman. To be the last living member of your family was difficult. I understood—I lived it. Be that as it may, a question still burned in the pit of my stomach.

How could I possibly help this woman?

The bubbling sensation of doubt rose in my throat like bile. At that moment, I wanted to run for the door. Except there was JoJo, with her little hand grasping firmly to my wrist. She looked at me with her full, alabaster smile and blue eyes wrinkled at the corners.

"Come this way, Miss Wyld. Ada likes to sit in east parlor by the window in the early evenin'."

As we entered the room, a beam of golden sunlight blinded me. Illuminated dust motes danced across it like summer fireflies at dusk. I squinted and used a hand to shade my eyes. That was when I first saw Miss Adalynn King.

The mistress of Kingsgrove looked much younger than her sixty years. Her hair was long and loose; it fell halfway down her back in thick silvery waves. She wore a summer dress that touched the floor and a light shawl over her shoulders. Her elegance and matured beauty could rival the muse of any fine, renaissance painting. When she turned toward us, her bright hazel eyes seemed to pierce right through me. I would never forget the lost look in them. It was as though her thoughts were listlessly wandering in some faraway place.

JoJo introduced me. "Ada, this is Miss Wyld. She's the young lady I told you 'bout. She'll be stayin' here to keep you company. Miss Wyld is an artist. Isn't that interestin'?"

I held out my hand in acknowledgment. The woman hesitated then eventually took it in hers. The moment was brief. Adalynn nodded ever so slightly then turned her back to us, facing the garden that grew outside the bay window. The twilight sun shadowed the woman's face, making her look severe and disenchanted. As if on cue, JoJo hooked her arm with mine and guided me out of the room.

"Miss King is shy at first," JoJo explained. "She's a recluse, you understand. The locals 'round here say things, but they leave her alone for the most part. The King family was wealthy and is still well respected in Willow Vale. The late Mr. King owned and operated the old paper mill before he passed. He was a family man and very good with his money. Ada's sittin' on a fortune, I reckon. It's a funny thing, all that money there for nothin', with no one to pass it on too. Ada never married. She never had any young ones of her own either. It was the same story with all her sisters. It's almost like them women were cursed and barren. It's a strange and sad thing." JoJo shrugged her small shoulders then gestured up toward the stairway.

"You mentioned that Miss King had an accident. Do you mind if I ask what happened?" The build-up of curiosity was too much to ignore.

"Ahh yes. The accident." JoJo sighed. "Poor thing almost drowned in the river that runs behind Kingsgrove. She was ten years old when it happened. Her mother found her on the riverbank half near dead, lookin' white as a ghost. Can you imagine! No one even knows how she ended up there. I'm sure as rain that she found herself by the pearly gates for a tick."

"That's terrible," I said, taken aback.

With her lips pressed together, JoJo nodded in agreement. "Well now, let's not talk about such unpleasant things. It's time to show you where you'll be stayin'. I'll see to Miss King for tonight, so that you can settle in."

We ascended the stairs. Then JoJo led me to the old servant's quarters in the west wing.

"I just changed the sheets and aired out the place," she said. "It's been quite some time since this old house has seen anyone besides Ada occupy its many rooms."

After giving me a gentle squeeze on the arm, JoJo left me by myself. I stood in the middle of the room and looked around. There was a double bed, draped in a heavy quilt, and an oak dresser pushed against the back wall. A writing desk was cornered next to the room's only window. The wood had been recently oiled and the drawers emptied. I was relieved to see a joining washroom, even with it being out-dated and about the size of a closet. A vintage clawfoot tub easily filled the space. For a moment, I grieved that there was no shower. At least it was private and smelled of lemons.

To quell the anxiety that gripped at my chest, I took a few deep breaths of fresh air. The wind had picked up, lifting the curtains and my hair along with it. Through the open window, I noticed the setting sun had painted the sky purple. I went in for a closer look and froze mid-step, for staring up at me was the King family cemetery—four headstones, each one marking the graves of Adalynn's older sisters.

From the upper floor it was easy to see what hid behind the willow tree. There were two large stone angels—a male and female counterpart. With imposing wings spread, their faces looked down in sorrow. Surely, they stood in memory of Mr. and Mrs. King. I swallowed the lump that swelled in my throat and shivered, despite the warm summer wind. The dead rested only a few strides away from my room. It was unsettling.

While watching the shadows in the yard grow with dusk, I was suddenly taken by surprise. As if to get my attention, a hand surely rested on my shoulder. I practically jumped out of my skin, only to turn and find I was still alone. My heart hammered in my chest and throat. Then I saw the curtain move with the wind, just as it had before.

It was the curtain. Right?

Yes, it *had* to be the curtain.

To shake off the uneasiness, I chose to settle in for the evening. By the time my car was unloaded and some clothes were unpacked, it was midnight. After catching a glimpse of my bloodshot eyes in the mirror, I decided to crawl into bed.

Outside, the crickets blared in the still of the night. However, the sounds that came from within Kingsgrove were much worse. In the late hours, the estate was alive with many creaks and cries. Being that it was so large and old, these sounds were normal, I reminded myself. Even still, I got up to turn the washroom light on before slipping back under the covers. With the sheets pulled up to my chin, I hummed softly to lull myself to sleep.

ROARS AND WHISPERS

That first night, I had dream—a terrible dream. It began with me high above the world looking down . . .

> *It was summer, and the air felt like freedom. I spread my arms to let the breeze seep between my fingers. It was harmless fun. After all, I was not alone. Someone was there. I could hear them calling my name.*
>
> *"Emilie. Emilie!"*
>
> *In a heartbeat, it was over. I was falling down, down, down, until the world swallowed me whole. The light vanished as I sank into the deep. There was no air— there was only fire. With lungs burning, my last breath escaped with the light and left me behind in the dark.*

Gasping out loud, I startled awake, eyes wide and burning.

Where was I? At first glance, everything was strange and unfamiliar. I rubbed the blur from my eyes and began to see the bits and pieces of me scattered about the room: a dream-catcher I made some years ago, a pallet with spackled layers of hardened paint, a dog-eared copy of Macbeth, and a tie-dyed pashmina, lying on the floor like a discarded rainbow.

It was *my* room. I lived and worked there.

As my thudding heart slowed, I found the clock on the wall. The hour hand was a few ticks away from six a.m. It was time to drag myself out of bed and face a new day.

The floor creaked with every step from the bedside to the wash-room where the clawfoot tub seemed to beckon me. I ran a bath, tossed my clothes aside, and tested the water with my toes. As the surface rippled, I purred in satisfaction and sank all the way in. My cheeks flushed from the delicious heat. It felt amazing. Soon, my body was lathered in suds of soap. Clusters of aromatic bubbles grew, and I popped a few of the iridescent domes with a fingertip.

After shampooing, I held my breath, closed my eyes tight, and dunked my head beneath the surface. As I worked the soap out of my hair, weaving my fingers between the strands, a flashback of the nightmare shocked my mind. My eyes flew open, and for one crazy second, I believed I was drowning! The air in my lungs escaped. Frantically, I gripped the edge of the tub and yanked myself out of the water, coughing violently. My wet hands rubbed and pressed against my eyes to relieve the soapy sting.

When the coughing ceased, I quickly finished bathing, making sure to keep my head above water the entire time. Only once the stopper was out and the tub emptied was I able to relax.

After towelling off, I looked at myself in the mirror above the pedestal sink. The glass was thin and waved slightly, distorting my face, which was sun-kissed from the drive the day before. The tan looked nice against the fairness of my hair and blue eyes. Normally, I did not wear any make-up. There was a tawny spray of freckles on my cheeks and nose. My nana always insisted that I never cover them up. My heart warmed at the memory of her holding my face in her hands. She looked at me with those wise, opal eyes of hers, and said my ashen hair and freckles were unique. She said I was different, because I was special. Whatever that meant, I was comfortable in my own skin, thanks to her.

Once dressed in an oversized bohemian-style blouse and a pair of denim cut-offs, the hunt for food and coffee was on. Thankfully, the large kitchen at Kingsgrove was easy enough to find. Next to the sink were some freshly washed dishes drying by the open window. It appeared that Adalynn had already had her breakfast, so I took it upon myself to prepare food and coffee for one. With a mug in one hand and a slice of toast in the other, I ventured out to the veranda.

It was a pretty summer day. I sat on the steps and happily drank from my steaming mug. The sound of rushing water could be heard from somewhere nearby. I closed my eyes to listen and soak in the day's first, hot rays of sun. There was a rustling to the right of the veranda. It was Miss King, quietly weeding her perennials in a large straw hat.

I called out. "Good morning, Adalynn."

Her head rose as my voice cut through the still of the garden. Looking effortlessly beautiful, the woman just stared as if she only just remembered I existed. Finally, she acknowledged me with a tiny nod of the head.

"Would you like any help with that?" I asked.

To my surprise, she smiled slightly and shook her head *no*. I was secretly relieved. We were strangers, and I was not sure how we were going to change that. Without words, where would we begin?

"All right. I'm going to take a look around, if you don't mind. Let me know if you need anything."

She motioned with her hand, as if to say *that's fine*, with a little smile still curled at the corner of her mouth. This might not be so bad after all, I thought. Hopefully, in time, things would get a better.

I ignored the itch of doubt, gnawing the back of my mind.

Being the first day on the job, there was no better time to explore the grounds at Kingsgrove. Right away, I looked around and sighed. The vast property was poorly maintained and wildly overgrown. As caretaker, cleaning it up was my responsibility. It was a lot of work. At least it would keep me busy, I resolved.

The sound of the river lured me to the back of the estate. Cicadas called out from their grassy haven as my feet parted the sea of weeds and wildflowers. I found the water's edge and stared at the wide, flowing current. Mrs. King found her youngest daughter half-drowned on that riverbank. The shocking image flashed in my mind. Trying to bury the unsettling thought, I crouched down and picked up a small twig as a distraction. Half-heartedly, I wrote my name in the soil, as if to make my mark. Perhaps it was to convince myself that I belonged.

At the last cursive stroke of the twig, the wind picked up and blew my hair madly around me. Amidst the sudden flurry, I heard someone say my name.

"Emilie . . ." It was hardly a whisper.

I stood up, frantically clawing the hair off my face. My eyes darted between the trunks and leafy boughs along the riverside. The wind gusted again, throwing leaves onto the water's surface. There was no one there. There was no one anywhere, except for Miss King, who was hunched over some lilies in the distance. It could not have been her. Adalynn did not speak. She had not since . . .

I turned back to face the river. It looked so deep and powerful.

Dark clouds rolled across the sky at an alarming rate. Before the rain came down, I decided to head back toward the house. I kept to the east side of the building to avoid the cemetery. My nightmare still lingered in the light of day, waiting to play tricks on my conscious mind. First, there was the bathtub then there was the whispery voice. It was enough to put anyone on edge. A cemetery was the last thing I wanted to see.

I passed behind Adalynn and saw her back stiffen. She did not acknowledge me and continued working in silence. I entered the house and set on exploring the main floor. The doors to the east parlor were left open. It was where JoJo had introduced me to Miss King the day before.

The room was dim, yet I could see well enough to look around. The walls were shelved and stacked with leather bound books. I ran my fingertips along the frayed spines and read some of the many titles: Charlotte Brontë's *Jane Eyre*, Charles Dickens' *Three Ghost Stories*, Wilkie Collins' *The Woman in White*, and Emily Brontë's *Wuthering Heights*. It was an extensive collection of classic fiction. There was also a complete set of encyclopaedias and a worn-out medical text of the human anatomy.

My eyes wondered around the room and rested on a large book that was left open on a desk. I walked over and sat on the stool before it. It was the Bible. Underlined in faded ink, was a passage.

Matthew 18:35 So also my heavenly Father will do to every one of you, if you do not forgive your brother from your heart.

I was not a religious person and was unschooled in scripture. Even still, it was difficult to say why anyone would highlight that particular passage. Taking care not to lose the page, I delicately flipped to the inside of the front cover. I thought of my grandmother's old Bible. It was a place where many families wrote each member's name and date-of-birth. It was true in this case. There, written in a very fine hand, was a list of Kings.

Jonathan King, June 18th, 1897
Evelyn King, February 14th, 1902

Violet King, January 20th, 1925
Alice King, March 3rd, 1928
Tabitha Rose King, August 2nd, 1931
Emma Rose King, August 2nd, 1931
Adalynn King, April 22nd, 1935

The names were faded, though still quite easy to read. I learned that Adalynn had twin sisters before her. It was interesting, yet something else intrigued me even more. There seemed to be a large space between Evelyn, the mother's name, and the first-born, Violet. Normally, it would have been overlooked without a second thought. So why couldn't I look away? Something was missing—I was sure of it. The empty space almost had an impression from where ink once touched the paper. Perhaps I was wrong. Perhaps the shadows in the room were playing tricks on me, as shadows often do. Squinting, I recounted the names. All seven were there. I reached to touch the page just as the floorboards creaked behind me. I jumped, which caused the stool to fall and tumble loudly on the hardwood floor. Standing there, in the center of the room, was Miss King. She looked at me with no expression on her stately face. I flipped back to the marked page in the Bible and awkwardly placed the chair in front of the desk.

My cheeks burned red. "I was just . . . uh . . . wondering if you wanted to read with me. Or I mean, wanted me to read to you?" I stammered. "I like your books. You have some of my favorites."

Ada seemed to let out a small silent chuckle, as she shook her head *no,* in response. Instead, she walked over to a basket of yarn, lifted it up to show me, and then left the parlor with it in tow. Shortly after, I found her outside knitting and rocking gently in the porch swing. The weather had turned, and it began to rain. While I stood by the front door, the sky lit up with lightning and a crackle of thunder followed. My nerves were so rattled that I pressed a hand to my chest in surprise.

As the sky poured on Willow Vale, the sensation of déjà-vu washed over me. I recalled a long-forgotten, stormy night as a young girl. When the thunder and lightning struck, my grandmother had made a game of it. I dressed up like a superhero, with a blanket tied around my neck and a feather in my hair. Together, we fought pretend monsters with a soup ladle and spatula. Instead of being afraid of the roar in the sky, I waited for it with a childlike anticipation.

The memory of my grandmother pierced right through my heart. I missed her. With a hand resting over my silver locket, I stepped out onto the veranda. Without thinking twice, I walked over to Adalynn and sat in a wicker chair by the swing. We stayed there for the rest of the afternoon and watched the storm in silence.

The downpour had faded into a steady rainfall by sunset. There was nothing better to do than explore, so I climbed the staircase to the east wing. Every hallway was dark and the electrical was ancient. I went from room to room, turning on lamps and feeling along the plaster walls for light switches.

As one empty bedroom flooded with light, I caught a glimpse of my own reflection. It stared back at me from an antique vanity mirror. A halo of blonde curls had frizzed above my forehead from the humidity. With no one to impress, I simply shot a sour look at my reflection, sighed, and turned away.

The sound of rain falling on the rooftop lured me over to the window. It was left open, and the air smelled clean and floral, but raindrops were spattered on the sill. I closed the pane and walked out into the hallway. The bedroom light spilled onto the floor and crept up the walls behind me. The shadows loomed and leered as I meandered through the corridor. The sensation of being followed was hard to ignore. Except I knew I was alone—apart from a grandfather clock ticking somewhere in the dark. I remembered hearing it the evening before. Its haunting chime echoed in the late hours of the night.

I found the clock at the end of the hall and stared up at its grandeur. Standing so close, I could hear all the gears clicking and rotating within. The brass pendulum swung hypnotically inside its home of ornate wood and glass. My thoughts drifted. The clock's stylized features and rhythmic purr had me mesmerized.

The spell broke by a sudden eerie creak. There was a door next to me. I stood paralyzed and watched it open . . . all on its own. An icy chill spilled down my spine as I dared to look in. A lace curtain, which glowed with moonlight, billowed in the wind like the gown of a banshee. Seeing that an open window was the culprit, I exhaled slowly to relieve the anxious grip on my chest.

A little girl's room was revealed as I turned on the light. There was pink and white lace throughout. A vintage teddy bear sat all worn and happy between the frilled pillows on the bed. Displayed in one corner was a pristine and lavish dollhouse. Framed silhouettes of little girls holding parasols and lollipops hung on the walls.

With a closer look, I noticed a pair of woman's slippers by the bed and a satin robe draped over a chair. Then I saw the straw-hat Miss King wore that very morning, resting on the foot of the bed. That was when I realized it was *her* room.

It seemed as if Adalynn had not changed a thing since she was a little girl. Why would she live that way? Kingsgrove had many rooms and bedchambers. She could have any one of them. At least, one that was more suitable for a grown woman. Instead, she chose a room meant for a child. Finding it very bizarre, I quickly shut the window and left. I turned off the remaining lights, blanketing the space behind me in darkness.

The eerie sensation of someone either watching me or following close behind had my nerves dancing. I hurried down to the main floor and found Miss King on the center landing. She was slowly making her way up the creaky steps. The woman looked tired and was likely heading to bed. Consequently, I said, "Goodnight," and did the same.

It was too early for sleep, so I lay on the bed with an open sketchbook. The pencil hit the paper, and before long, the scrawled lines came together. It was a raven in flight with a clock-face crushed inside its sharp talons. Loose gears and tiny screws fell into an abyss of spiralling clouds.

I had no idea where the image came from. It was possible that Kingsgrove had brought out my darker side. The raven was so severe and mysterious, but the image was captivating. My hand seemed to have a mind of its own. The pencil moved with ease as I spent the rest of the evening bringing life to the blank, white page.

TOUCHED

With a flash, my unconscious mind opened up to another disturbing dream . . .

I was a little girl again. My long, blonde hair was loose and tangled from playing outside. While sitting on the lawn of my grandmother's yard, I could even feel the grass tickle my thin, bare legs.

The midday sun was blinding. My nana stood before me. Her black silhouette was traced in a halo of light. I tried calling out to her, but when my mouth opened nothing escaped. I tried again—silence. Hot tears poured down my sunburnt cheeks. I stood up, squeezed my eyes shut, and screamed a desperate, empty scream. She just stood there, motionless, as I clawed at her dress and crumpled to the ground.

My eyes shot open. I was wide-awake in an instant. Something wasn't right.

The tears from my nightmare were real. My face was still damp with them. The pain I dreamt was so vivid that my every nerve was standing at attention.

Skin crawling, I tried to focus my eyes, but it was too dark. I had forgotten to turn on the washroom light before bed and regretted it deeply at that moment. It was too quiet, as if every sound had been sucked right out of the space. The air was so thick. It was suffocating. My chest tightened as panic set in, making me short of breath. Even as the soft glow of the moon revealed I was alone, I knew something was not right.

Someone was there, watching me.

Frozen in shock, I felt the weight of an unseen mass press down on the bed. The sheets moved and tightened next to me. My heart stopped. Was I imagining things? My mind was surely playing tricks on me.

My arms quivered as I sat up. All my muscles were tense and my body was gripped with fear. I froze as a growing energy encumbered me. It was electric. The tiny hairs rose on my neck and arms as the sensation heightened. It reached an intensity that was virtually unbearable. At the peaking moment, I felt something rest against my cheek. A disembodied hand was touching my tearstained face.

Terror invaded my body like venom. I squeezed my eyes closed and gritted my teeth to stifle the scream welling up inside.

A choked whimper escaped my lips.

Immediately, the heaviness fled from the room. The silence broke. Even the ticking clock could be heard once again. The presence I felt was gone. I was gratefully relieved of the static grip on my body. On impulse, I jumped up and turned on the bedside lamp.

Light flooded the room.

I rubbed my blurry eyes then stared at the empty bed.

"This is crazy," I said out loud. My voice sounded so small— so young.

My eyes were still adjusting to the light as they focused on the clock. It was three a.m. I hugged my shivering arms. Going back to sleep was out of the question, instead I just stared longingly at the bedroom door. A war between fear and irrationality raged on in my heart. Time stood still as my head veered with indecision. The ghostly touch was mind-bending, making it impossible to grasp onto a single rational thought. In the end, I reluctantly sat on the edge of the bed. After a few deep breaths, I found the strength to get back under the covers. They were cold and unwelcoming.

Any other person would have run for the door. They would escape to a safe place. They would go home. Where would I go? Kingsgrove was my *only* home. It was supposed to be my safe place.

I gripped the sheets as it finally hit me. I was lost, and there was no one to find me.

My grandmother was dead. She was all I had growing up—she was my protector. Even up to the final hours, her spirit was mighty. My stubbornness was inherited from her, and the desire to leave at that moment was just as strong as the desire to stay. My heart and mind were tormented. Something was telling me that Kingsgrove was where I was meant to be. The fear was irrelevant. The estate was so rich with its own past. The artist in me could hardly resist the mysteries it held. Plus, my job, the main reason I was here, was to help Adalynn. She too, was lost. She needed to find the little girl that was swept away by the river years ago.

The door seemed to pulsate in the glow of my bedside lamp. It would be so easy to jump in the Trans Am and hit the road, but I was tired of running. I came to Willow Vale with pockets full of freedom and independence. Nothing could take that away from me. I would not let it.

With great difficulty, the decision was made. I would stay for as long as possible, assuming nothing else happened, of course. Any unseen force would have to forget about me, or I would have to forget about *it*. As fearless as that sounded, deep inside I knew the truth. My resilience was nothing more than a foolish lie.

My thoughts were so overrun with *things that go bump in the night* that I had to get out of bed in search of a distraction. I finished unpacking and started to turn the room into a place of my own. Bit by bit, my personal touch transformed the empty space. In some way, it helped anchor me to the house—it forced me to belong.

As a final touch, I ripped the clock-crushing raven out of my sketchbook and tacked it to the wall. With a slow spin, I looked at the room around me and actually smiled. The house was truly a beautiful place. It was elegantly designed and detailed with loving intent. The property and everything that Willow Vale had to offer was inspiring. I imagined the Kings were very happy in their home. Even the servant's quarters were just as lovely as JoJo had said. It was the nicest room that I had ever had . . . besides the view. Yet, even *it* had an eerie sort of beauty.

I looked through the window at the grounds below. Daytime had finally arrived, though the sun was hidden by an overcast sky. The grey sheet of clouds darkened the cemetery below, making it especially ominous. Seeing the marked stones made me wonder which King, other than Adalynn, still roamed the halls at night. Perhaps *all* the spirits of the deceased family were haunting their beloved property. Hopefully, I was completely wrong and there was no such thing as ghosts. Perhaps I was over-tired and had imagined the entire thing. I liked that idea, because it was logical—it made sense.

I tried desperately to forget the late-night encounter, though my efforts were weak. The frightening event replayed over and over in my mind, coiling my stomach with anxiety. Something was in my bed. It touched me! My cheek still tingled from the caress of ghostly fingers. The electricity that filled the room was remarkable. That energy—that unearthly sensation—was too hard to forget.

My mind was reeling, and I started to feel thoroughly unhinged. I had to shake it off and swallow the fear. It was morning, and time to start a new day. Being that I was traumatized, mentally and physically, I took a very short bath, dressed in record time, and promptly left the room.

It was early, and Adalynn still had herself tucked away in the east wing. I put the kettle on to boil then found eggs and bacon in the fridge. Convinced food would cure my knotted stomach, I started making breakfast for two. The smell filled the room, and I zoned out to the sizzling skillet. As the kettle shrilled and spattered with bubbles and steam, the atmosphere in the room changed. Someone was behind me. I felt a tinge of panic and turned swiftly to find Miss King.

"Good morning," I called over the kettle's shrill, smiling in relief. Adalynn did not seem to notice the spatula shaking in my hand. The woman just nodded my way then emptied the kettle into the teapot. I filled our plates with food and carried them into the dining room. A moment later, Miss King joined me with two steaming teacups in hand. We sat across from each other and started to eat. The utensils clanked and scraped loudly on our plates. The sound was painfully amplified by all the awkward silence.

My lips parted to speak, but the words froze in my throat. I took a deep breath and shifted in my seat. How was I going to have a one-way conversation with this woman? It was not for a lack of interesting topics to choose from, for many questions troubled my mind. All of which were about Kingsgrove, and its many hidden marvels.

I wanted to know if she, too, was haunted in the night. Did the wind ever whisper her name? Had she ever felt a presence follow so close that she felt its breath on the back of her neck? If only she could tell me something, anything, to subdue the anxiety that consumed me.

My nana used to say that I had an overactive imagination. Regardless of all that, I had never experienced anything quite so . . . paranormal. As much as I wanted to believe that it was merely a dream, I knew it was much more than that.

I looked at Adalynn's face as she concentrated on her breakfast. She looked nothing like my grandmother, who was less refined. Even though Miss King had no voice, her presence was eminent and spoke volumes. She carried with her a profound sense of mystery. My nana lived simply and was comfortable, like a fleece blanket—like home. Adalynn seemed appeased with her seclusion. A part of me still felt like I was intruding on her quiet existence.

As each minute ticked by, the silence grew, filling the room like an impalpable smog. Searching desperately for anything to say, I realized Adalynn knew nothing about me. After all, I was not from Willow Vale. Miss King deserved to know the stranger living in her home.

Reluctantly, I parted my lips again to speak. "It's so quiet here. I'm not used to it, but it's kind of nice. In the city, when the sun goes down, the lights come on and the noise never stops." Adalynn's eyes met mine, and seemed almost present for the first time. Trying to ignore the anxious twinge in my gut, I stammered on. "My mother always wanted to live in the south. I was never sure why until now."

Before long, my guts were spilled and my past was laid raw and bare before Miss King. She knew then all there was to tell about my mother . . . Hannah. What came over me, I will never know. Until then, Hannah's story was one I kept locked away in the deepest part of me. Even though we never met, her memory was mine to keep and no one else's. My nana said that we were connected and on the day she died, Hannah's spirit became a part of my own. As crazy as it sounded, I believed her. Over twenty years had passed since her apartment caught fire. At the time, I was still growing inside of her. She died, and somehow, my life was spared. All I had was a shoebox of faded Polaroids to know her by. As for my father, he left before my mother's sudden death. She never told anyone his name—she never had the chance. He was, and will forever be, a stranger to me.

After Hannah's story, I shared the highs and lows of my life before Kingsgrove. My brief recollection of childhood was full of my grandmother's guidance and good intentions. I expressed how much her presence was missed in my life. After she died there was no one left, so I moved out of the suburbs and into the city. The city was where I enrolled in art school and where I had my first, failed relationship.

While the stories bled together and left my lips with candor, Adalynn just sat and listened, only looking down periodically to sip her tea. Little by little, her far-away look dissipated and she seemed quite engaged. My own anxiety began to unwind as well. Speaking to the woman actually felt good, even though her life story was likely more exciting than my own.

Eventually, I stopped talking and looked into her hazel eyes. "I hope you don't mind me staying here. I'll do my best to help out, and at the very least, I hope we can become friends." I was stunned and abashed by my own honesty. Miss King reached across the table and kindly tapped her hand on mine. The tiny gesture melted a little more of the fear away.

Was it possible that I needed her as much as she needed me?

Miss King rose from her seat and began to clear the table. I took the plate gently from her hand and insisted on cleaning up. She reluctantly conceded, then left me alone in the dining room. I took the dishes into the kitchen and started to fill the sink with hot, soapy water. The suds blossomed into little frothy clouds.

As steam hazed the air, my thoughts drifted back to the one-sided conversation with Miss King. Although it was nice to open up for once, it left me feeling vulnerable. Even in the light of day, I could imagine an unseen entity listening and learning all my insecurities. Dread prickled across my skin, and I shot a quick glance over both shoulders.

What did I expect to find? Did I actually think that the old house was haunted? Was the King's residual energy still reliving the days gone by? Or was something trying to scare me with intent?

Was I in danger?

More importantly, was I really entertaining the idea of ghosts?

My paranoia was leading me down that fearful path. I forced myself to ignore my fears and focus my energy toward sweeping and dusting the old estate. It was easy enough, for the many rooms were teeming with antique furniture and knickknacks. I took my time examining each and every ornamental piece. A porcelain poodle here, an oil lamp there; everything was faded and burnished to perfection.

There were many black and white photos hung and propped on display throughout house, most depicting elegantly dressed young women posed with an attitude of sophistication. One of my favorite pictures was of the twins: Tabitha Rose and Emma Rose. The girls looked to be in their late teens at the time. Their dark beauty was mirrored perfectly in likeness. My own fairness reflected back in the glass. In the great room, there was a large picture in a gilded frame above the fireplace. It was a wedding portrait of Mr. and Mrs. King. They stood together, frozen in a sepia-toned vignette. Mr. King stood proud, chest out, with a striking moustache on his upper lip. Mrs. King had her dark hair twisted up in a crown of braids, bejeweled in flowers. The newlyweds looked young and happy, holding each other close.

Would *I* ever feel that drawn to another? It was hard to imagine. Much like the Kingsgrove estate, my heart was isolated. Clearly, my last relationship suffered because of it. I refused to let him in for different reasons—the most important one being *fear.*

After my grandmother died, there was no one left. There was no one to catch me when I stumbled, no one to take my hand and guide my path, no one to hold me when words were not enough, and there was no more unconditional love. Her death shook me and threw me until I chose to disconnect from anyone and everyone. Life was easier that way. I found comfort in relying on only myself. Before Kingsgove, it was easy for me to stand alone in the world.

So what changed?

While hanging onto every last strand of my proud independence, a new feeling threatened to pull me down. Seeing the newlyweds embrace above the fireplace mantel, with love still fresh in their eyes, left me feeling . . . empty.

To shake off all the uneasy thoughts, I immediately went back to work, sweeping soot into the hearth. Once the main floor was primped and polished, I found myself deep in the west wing. There was not much on that side of the estate, except for the servant's quarters and a few rooms meant for storage. I entered one and found a number of boxes stacked along the walls. Curiosity got the best of me, and I lifted a few of the cardboard lids. Kingsgrove was a mystery to me; I couldn't help myself.

Disappointingly, all I found were old documents from the paper mill. There was nothing but box after box of out-dated invoices and receipts. A couple of steamer trunks sat off in one dark corner. I opened them partway and found only aged linens that smelled of mothballs. Needless to say, there was nothing too exciting. I gave up the search and left after sweeping the dust away.

Shortly after, I came across a small hallway that I had overlooked before. It led to a single doorway. The corridor was dismal and lacked the comfort of daylight. Fear lingered and gnawed in the corner of my mind. Intrigue took over, and I found myself gripping the doorknob. The brass was so cold in my hand. I pushed the door open and it creaked loudly in protest.

Before me was a large bedroom shrouded in darkness. The heavy curtains were drawn and the air was thick and musty. I felt for the light switch with no success. I hurried over to the window and tore open the drapes. The gloomy day offered very little light. Nevertheless, I saw the impressive, four-poster bed that filled the space. Its wooden frame was thick with dust and nothing but cobwebs decorated the furniture throughout. Even the few picture frames hanging on the walls were empty.

It seemed so strange to me. For no reason at all, a rush of heartbreak came over me. The bedroom felt like a sad, forgotten place. Being so large and adorned, no servants would have stayed there. All the members of the King family slept in the east wing.

So, whose bedroom was it?

Out of nowhere, my breath appeared like a puff of smoke before my lips. A chill passed through the air and my body froze up. Icy shivers began at the nape of my neck and quivered down to the tips of my toes. Something or someone was there.

I was not alone.

In an instant, a vibration began beneath my feet. The tremor spread across the floor and crept up the walls. The room came alive with a vibrant energy. In disbelief, I slowly pressed my hands and cheek to the wall. I felt the tremble with my palms and saw the picture frames shake and clamor. My eyes widened as panic began to set in. The rapid beat of my heart and my heaving chest nearly caused me to faint. I pushed myself off the wall and stepped back. The vibration immediately stopped.

"Okay. What the hell was that?" I whimpered. My adrenaline was pumping and my legs could no longer hold me. I sat with my back against the wall and gripped my hair at the scalp. My eyes scanned the room wildly.

Was it a small earthquake? I had my doubts. To be honest, I was starting to believe that *something* was out to get me.

✗ ✗ ✗

That evening, I tuned into the old radio in Mr. King's former office. I expected to hear something about the rumble I felt that afternoon when the weather update followed the local news. The announcer did predict a severe thunderstorm for later that week, yet nothing but overcast skies and sticky temps in the meantime. I tapped a pencil impatiently on the desk until the staticky southern voice wrapped up the segment, mentioning nothing out of the ordinary, and a country song took over the airwave.

The radio did not explain away the quake that shook the old estate. Even so, it did not mean the anomaly was supernatural. There had to be another logical explanation. But at that point, there were only two options. I could dwell on it, or pretend it never happened. There was no reason for me to visit the strange bedroom again. Sadness radiated from those four empty walls. I wanted to forget it even existed. Unfortunately, that was easier said than done.

The room was only a few steps away from where I laid my head at night. No wonder my dreams had turned into nightmares. With a graveyard on one side and *that bedroom* on the other—nightmares were inevitable.

I rubbed my twitching eyelid and began to doodle on a small pad of paper. I drew a pair of eyes. They began to take life with every stroke of lead. As I formed and shaded, they looked back at me with heartache. They seemed to plead for help. I swiftly folded the paper and tucked it in the back pocket of my denim shorts. Lynyrd Skynyrd's *Free Bird* was playing on the radio when I turned it off.

It was time to leave the office in search of Miss King. The first place I looked was the east parlor. She was sitting on a loveseat at the far end of the room. She expertly worked her knitting needles, and a woolly creation gathered in her lap. An old record player spun a classical song that I did not recognize. The light was dim and the vinyl's static sound made the air come alive and thickened the atmosphere. Adalynn did not look up as I entered the room. I sat in the window seat and admired the crescent moon. A light breeze flowed through the dark garden, just beyond my reach. The blossoms danced and bowed to the rhythm of the music.

"It's very peaceful here." I ran my hand down the delicate, lace curtain. "I've never lived in a place quite like this. It must have been a wonderful home to share with your family. I'm sure you miss them."

She nodded in agreement.

A minute or two passed before I found the courage to continue. I positioned my body toward her in preparation and took a deep, quiet breath. My next words were spoken with a careful consideration. "Although, in some ways, it feels like they're *still here*." It almost sounded like a question. I looked at Adalynn with intensity. Her head popped up and her eyes widened momentarily. It was only for a split second, but I saw it. My heart skipped a beat. She quickly regained composure and continued knitting.

Was that it? Was *that* my answer? Did Adalynn also feel an unseen presence in the house?

I watched her complete a row then put down her knitting tools. She stood up and crossed the room to the bookcase. Adalynn removed a small, clothbound pocketbook and brought it over. After placing it in my hands, she returned to her place on the loveseat. I glanced at the cover. It was a very old copy of the Brothers Grimm's *Hansel and Gretel*. I gave her a confused look.

Was she serious—a children's book?

With a sweep of her hand, she motioned for me to go ahead and read.

The chords of Tchaikovsky filled the parlor as I made my way through the story with ease. The print was large, and significant moments were elaborately illustrated. When the witch lured both brother and sister into her candy house, I heard Adalynn shift in her seat. I paused and glanced up to see a pair of hazel eyes pierce right through me. Her lurid stare was discomforting. I went on to finish the story then rested the book on my lap. We looked at each other from across the room. Was I was missing something? She was waiting for me to fill in the blanks. The problem was I did not know where to start.

I opened my mouth to ask if something was a matter. Before the words could come out, the needle fell from the edge of the record. To cut the tension, I went over and put on another album. The *Moonlight Sonata* resonated throughout. I held the book to my chest and turned to find Adalynn heading out of the room. She hid a yawn with her hand as she passed by.

"Goodnight Miss King. Sleep well," I said, knowing the moment was lost.

The only response I received was the sound of slippers shuffling off into the dark.

Left alone with my thoughts, I looked down at cover of *Hansel and Gretel*. At first glance, the old book seemed insignificant—the story of how a brother and sister outsmarted and survived a wicked witch. It was nothing but a fairy-tale, so why did Adalynn's face say otherwise?

It was becoming so clear to me that Kingsgrove was veiled in secrets waiting to be uncovered. Unfortunately, the only person who would know anything was Miss King. Did the woman with no voice have all the answers locked inside? There was a mystery left untold, without a doubt. Something was hiding in the shadows, and either I was about to find *it*, or *it* was about to find me.

THE DEVIL'S EMPORIUM

A meadowlark's song woke me the next morning. I had managed, after drinking two steaming cups of camomile tea and tracing the wallpaper pattern with my eyes, to sleep dead until daybreak. The dreamless night felt like heaven. It lifted my spirit and unravelled the anxiety that twisted in my gut.

My morning started with a hot bath, where I soaked and relished in all my lotions and potions. After washing from head to tippy-toe, I got out and dried my hair by the open window. Droplets of water trailed down my body as the gentle breeze cooled my heated skin.

I dug through my clothes and decided on a white summer dress with an embroidered trim. It was perfect outfit for a hot summer day in the Deep South. The skirt lifted weightlessly at the knee as I did a playful twirl before leaving the room. I practically glided all the way to the kitchen in search of Miss King, but found a note on the counter instead.

Emilie,
I'll be needing you to drive into town today.
Please go to the Willow Vale General Store (You can't miss it)
Ask for Louanne Carmichael and tell her I sent you.
Thank you dear.
—JoJo

I drank my coffee and ate in haste before slipping on a pair of flip-flops. I skipped down the front steps of Kingsgrove and hopped into the Trans Am. It was like a furnace and the seat stung the backs of my thighs. I rolled the windows down, cranked the radio, and drove off. A hot draft poured in and did little to thin the sultry air.

My hair curled in the humidity and tickled my face with the breeze. I held back the messy strands and smiled contently. It felt so good to have a quiet night, free from both disturbing dreams and ghostly encounters. The drive down Kings Lane was a peaceful distraction. That was until the bright woodland turned into a dark and shady swamp. How I overlooked such a place on the drive in was beyond me.

Water drowned the forest floor and crept up the edge of roadside. The dirt lane sunk dangerously low, and was one bad storm away from flooding. The ruts, potholes, and roots were hard enough to navigate as it was. There was no other option than to drive slow and marvel at the sodden landscape. I studied how the light pushed through the treetops and painted itself on the murky water. A grove of bald cypress trees reflected off the calm, black surface. Their impressive trunks stood immersed in the everglade and their branches were heavy with moss. Matted tendrils wafted, ever so slightly, in the almost non-existent breeze. It was downright eerie. Even the sun-bleached roots of fallen trees reached from the water like the gnarled fingers of a skeleton.

Thankfully, the shady swamp was soon forgotten as the backwoods turned into the suburbs of Willow Vale. There were endless rows of picket fences and trees blossoming with crisp white magnolias. Young children jumped happily through lawn sprinklers while their parents gathered under porch fans, sipping sweet tea—anything to find relief from relentless heat.

The downtown core was quaint and manicured. All the old buildings along the main street were well preserved with all the original architectural details still intact. The road was cobblestone and the sidewalks were decorated with potted flowers, benches, and iron streetlamps. It was charming. I could hardly wait for a chance to look around.

JoJo had said that the *Willow Vale General Store* was hard to miss, and she was right. I found it with no trouble and parked nearby. As I stepped out to feed the meter, a small shop across the street caught my eye and stopped me dead in my tracks. A thick velvet curtain hung in the window, blocking the view inside from passer-byers. The sign above read, *The Eventide Emporium—Curiosities and Alchemy.*

I would have gone in, except the sign on the entrance was flipped to *Closed.* To be fair, it was early. Surely, the demand for strange novelties and silly love potions was low at that time of the morning. Even I had more important things to do than satisfy a strange curiosity.

A moment later, I stood facing the general store. The exterior was a patchwork of signs, both new and old. The veranda was stocked with fresh produce and a wide variety of household goods. I climbed the front steps and went inside through the open doors. The clapping sound of my flip-flops announced my entry unceremoniously.

"Well, well. Look what we have here," said a raspy, female voice. I turned to find an older woman sitting in a plastic patio chair. She was round and red-faced with curlers coiled tightly to her scalp. Her forehead and upper lip shone with sweat despite the small fan blowing directly on her. Resting in the woman's lap was an old rusty-eyed poodle. The little dog panted and observed me with a look of indifference.

"Hello. Are you Louanne Carmichael?"

"That all depends on whose askin'." She had a guarded look on her face, but I could detect the hint of humor in her eyes.

I reached up to touch my locket and felt the tiny hawk under my thumb. "My name is Emilie," I said. "JoJo Peters sent me on behalf of Miss Adalynn King." Louanne's face softened and she revealed a large, denture-filled smile.

"Ahhh. You must be the young woman JoJo was tellin' me 'bout last week. I knew you weren't from 'round here. That head of bright hair stands out like a sore thumb." I could feel my cheeks flush, and it wasn't from the heat. "Would you look at that there dress?" She went on. "In my younger days I could wear dresses like that. Of course mine weren't quite so short."

Louanne's backhanded remark took me by surprise. I subconsciously tugged the hem at the back of my dress.

"Cute dog." It was all I could think to say to change the subject.

"His name is Boo-Radley, and right now he's making me hotter than a billy goat's ass in a pepper patch." She shooed the poodle from her lap and wiped her damp brow with the back of her hand. My eyes must have been as wide as saucers in reaction the words that flew from Louanne's mouth. "Phew. Now that's a whole lot better. I'll call my husband 'round to help you, dear." Instead of getting up, she turned her face, closed her eyes, and yelled at the top of her raspy voice, "Hollis!" It made me jump. Even Boo-Radley's ears flattened as he hid his face with a curly paw. She turned back to me and said, "I swear that man's as useful as an ashtray on a scooter."

A laugh escaped me, and I quickly stifled it with my hand. I could not decide if I disliked or completely adored this woman.

Eventually, Hollis Carmichael appeared. He was balding, with rosy cheeks and a drinking man's nose. A pair of thick black suspenders hugged his ample belly. He grunted at Louanne, as if to ask what she wanted. "Gather up an order for Miss King. The usual," she instructed. He nodded and started filling a basket with food and supplies. The old woman turned back to me and asked, "So dear, how you likin' Willow Vale?"

"So far, it's lovely. I'm looking forward to doing a little more exploring," I said, most politely. "Speaking if which, I just passed by *The Eventide Emporium*. Do you know anything about the place?" The question just slipped right out. For some reason, the curiosity burned in the back of my mind. Louanne seemed like the type of lady who enjoyed a good gossip. Since her store was just down the road, I figured there was no one better to ask.

"Now, you listen here. Steer clear of that place if you know what's good for you. It's owned by Scarlet Eventide. Her grandmother was Olivia Eventide. Olivia was rumored to practice the Voodoo. Now, I don't believe in all that hocus-pocus, I just think it's mighty dangerous to align yourself with the Devil! Besides, that Scarlet has her nose so high in the air she could drown in a rainstorm. No one even knows who her father was. Can you believe it? Same story goes for her mother. What a scandal!"

Louanne enjoyed a good scandal, I imagined.

The old woman looked at her husband and snapped. "Hollis! Miss King prefers brown bread, not the white stuff." Mr. Carmichael grumbled miserably then pawed a loaf of whole-wheat bread off the shelf. Louanne turned back to me and lowered her voice. "That man is four quarters short of a dollar, I always say. He couldn't pour piss out of a boot with the instructions written on the heel." I chuckled and began to feel sorry for poor old Hollis.

Mr. Carmichael brought over a large, brown paper bag that was filled to the brim. I patted myself down and realized I had forgotten to bring money with me. "Shoot. I have no way to pay you."

"Hush yer mouth! You needn't worry about such things. Miss King has an account. It's all taken care of." Relieved, I said my thanks then waved goodbye to the Carmichaels.

By the time I dropped off the shopping bag in my car, I was fixated on the name Eventide. The word *Voodoo* was flashing bright neon in my mind. I looked back toward the emporium and noticed the sign had since been flipped to *Open*. What luck! My decision not to heed Mrs. Carmichael's warning was simple. After all, what harm would it do?

Beckoned by intrigue, I pushed open the door to the shop. A chime of little brass bells declared my entrance. The air was refreshing with a heavy hit of patchouli. I twisted my hair up to the feel the cool relief at my neck. As if out of thin air, a tall Cimmerian beauty appeared before me. Feeling unusually self-conscious, I let my hair fall and smiled awkwardly up at her.

"Welcome, Miss Wyld of Kingsgrove." Her voice was velvety smooth. She looked a few years older then I, perhaps in her early thirties. The woman was slender and dangerously sleek. She had an ink-black veil of hair and intelligent, grey eyes that were skilfully shadowed in charcoal.

"How would you know that?" I was taken aback.

"It's a small town, my dear Miss Wyld. Full of eager gossips and idle chatter," she replied.

"And you are?" I asked.

"Pardon my rudeness. I'm Scarlet Eventide." Her smile was sugary sweet. "Please come in and look around. If you have any questions, do not hesitate to ask."

My first question came quickly. It was hard to ignore the large, black birdcage hanging next to the counter. Perched within was a real live raven. "That's an interesting pet." I walked towards the animal. Its oily feathers shone brilliantly. The bird's beady eye was locked on me as I approached. "Why a raven?" I had to know.

"Let's just say, she's a part of the family." Scarlet's smile was abiding and her gaze intense.

"Interesting," I said politely while distancing myself from the bird's creepy stare.

I began exploring all the eccentricities of the dimly lit shop. In one corner, there was a curio cabinet filled with crude, handmade dolls. There was an assortment of shapes, sizes, and colors for an easy match to any helpless victim.

"Do you have any enemies, Miss Wyld?"

I giggled. "Not yet, Miss Eventide." I shot her a sly look.

"I see," she simply replied. We regarded each other for a moment. The energy between us was charged like two negative ends of a magnet. We were in complete contrast from each other. Even in appearance, Scarlet was dark and I was light. She looked at me, like a wildcat assessing an adversary before a fight. There was no explanation for it. We had only just met.

In an attempt to ignore Scarlet, I focused my attention to the shelves along the back wall. They were stockpiled with bottles and packets holding many strange components. Some were topped off with powder and some with liquid. There were also sacks of dried flowers and herbs. I saw what appeared to be hair, bones, and even teeth. Some of the labels read Powered Sulphur, Rose Oil, Brick Dust, Spanish Moss, Black Pepper Oil, Valerian Root, Drive-Away Salt, and Bat's Blood.

On another wall, there was nothing but books. There were texts on everything from incantations and spells, alchemy 1O1, and southern superstitions, to do-it-yourself Voodoo dolls. Both Scarlett and her raven watched me incessantly as I browsed.

"Are you looking to cast any enchantments yourself, Miss Wyld?" she asked me. "I have a fool-proof love spell that I could prepare for you. Do you have any young men you wish to charm?"

I laughed out loud. "No thank you, Miss Eventide. You seem to forget that I live at Kingsgrove where there are no young men. I've only been in Willow Vale for a few days. So far, the only man I've met is Hollis Carmichael. I highly doubt he's available for *charming*."

Scarlet looked down at me with her cloying smile still intact. "Have you seen our collection of talismans?" She guided me over to a glass display case. It was full of amulets and jewellery that were etched with tiny, foreign symbols.

"I'm really not that interested in purchasing anything today. I don't even have any money with me." I looked at her with a mock sense of disappointment. Scarlet ignored me and positioned herself behind the cabinet, unlocked it, and reached in to retrieve a tiny box. She opened the lid to reveal a small dark jewel with a blood-red center. Using her indigo-painted fingernails, she pinched the stone from its case. Scarlet came back around the display and stood in front of me.

In one swift motion, she reached up and rested my locket in the palm of her free hand. "What a treasure." She raised her other hand and displayed the tiny jewel between her thumb and forefinger. "Think of this as a welcome present. It will offer you safe guidance." Before I could refuse, she opened the locket, placed the stone in the empty compartment, and snapped it shut.

"I can't accept this," I said, backing away from her. Miss Eventide had caught me completely off guard.

"Nonsense! It's just a small token. Think of it as a thank-you for your charity toward our beloved Miss King." It was hardly charity. Adalynn was wealthy and very capable. Besides, I was being paid to live there.

Scarlet hushed all my protests and showed me to the exit. "Don't hesitate to visit us again. It was a pleasure to meet you." Before I knew it, she ushered me right out the door and onto the street. As I stepped outside, a wall of dense heat blasted me in the face. The drastic change in temperature left me lightheaded and unbalanced. I walked slowly on unsteady feet toward my car.

On the drive back to Kingsgrove, I was completely on-edge. No matter how hard I tried, I could not shake the feeling. My visit to *The Eventide Emporium* was very strange. Scarlet Eventide was far too shrewd and empowered. The woman acted as if she knew me before we even met.

I had never experienced the Voodoo culture before that day. Was it even real? I knew too little to answer that question with sincerity. Believing in Voodoo had never occurred to me before. However, with all the peculiar things that were happening, I was starting to think that *anything* was possible.

✗ ✗ ✗

JoJo and Adalynn were drinking tea and playing cards in the kitchen when I walked in. Ada sat in silence as JoJo prattled on about random scandals and meaningless drama. JoJo spotted me and forced down a mouthful of tea. "Well, hello dear! How have you been getting along so far?"

"Hello ladies. I've been doing just fine, thank you." I placed the paper shopping bag down on the counter.

"And how do you like Kingsgrove? Have you settled in okay?"

My eyes shot to Adalynn before responding. She did not look up from her hand of cards. She did not even move. Miss King was likely waiting, just as JoJo, for my answer.

I could have told them about the nightmares, the whispering, and the inexplicable force that stalked me. I could have told them that I thought the house was haunted . . . but I didn't.

"It's a fascinating place. I've settled in just fine, thanks for asking."

The small nurse appeared delighted. "I'm so pleased to hear that. You're just like a breath of fresh air 'round here." She winked at me then continued her one-sided conversation with Miss King. I listened in, half-heartedly, as I unpacked and prepared lunch. There were all the fixings to make ham sandwiches and fruit salad. After serving the ladies, I took my meal out to the veranda.

I finished eating and settled into the lush pillows on the porch swing. With the gentle rocking and a full stomach, I dozed off and started dreaming . . .

Two strong arms cradled my wet, limp body. My clothes were twisted so tightly around me, it was strangulating. I tried to open my eyes to see the young man that held me close. There was only darkness. My eyelids were so heavy—so very heavy and weak.

The unseen person was hauling me desperately through the woods. He was gasping for breath between each heart-wrenching cry. As he ran, branches tore at my arms and legs like claws reaching out to take me from him. At one point, he lost his footing and we fell to the earth. The young man dissolved into tears as he attempted to gather me in his lap. So badly, I wanted to reach up and comfort him. Even though I was dirty and broken, there was no pain. I wanted to tell him that everything was okay, but I couldn't move.

He rocked me in his arms and wailed. "No, Emilie! You can't be dead. You can't!"

But I was dead—cold and dead in his arms.

MASKS AND MONSTERS

My eyelids flickered then opened. The nightmare was over, but something was not quite right. For some reason, I felt strange—I felt disoriented and displaced.

With a jolt, I realized the porch swing was gone. Instead of sleeping on the veranda, I found myself on the riverbank with one bare foot ankle-deep in the cold water. In shock, I lifted it out and slid myself away from the edge.

Why was I there? Did I sleepwalk?

The current was ruthless, nearly claiming one victim already. What would have happened if more than a foot had ended up in the river?

I hugged my knees close to my chest.

The dream was so real that it shook me to the bone. The young man that carried me was a stranger, but in the dream, I knew him. Even with my eyes wide open, the connection to him was undeniable. The thought of dying in his arms was too much to bear.

I stood up and brushed the dirt off my dress. The day was still feverishly warm, and my skin felt unclean and sticky with sweat. I walked carefully back to the house. The grass was hot on the soles of my feet. How did I manage to go all that way, barefoot, and not wake up?

I was coming apart at the seams. Nothing made sense anymore.

The warm smell of noodle casserole filled the house when I came through the door. I no longer heard JoJo's sweet southern accent and assumed she had gone home. Adalynn was likely making dinner, so I avoided the kitchen and went up to my room.

I slipped out of my dress and stood naked in the middle of the bathroom floor. I half expected there to be scratches all over my body, like in the dream. Instead, I found only dried mud on my feet and a few small twigs in my hair.

After taking a cool bath, I pulled the plug and sat with my cheek resting on one knee. The twirling water vanished down the drain, taking the dirt from my body away with it. I lifted myself out of the empty tub and carefully dried my hair and skin.

I was shell-shocked and lost. It was like solving a puzzle with too many of the pieces missing. My sanity was slipping away, and I had to get a grip. There was only one thing that could give me refuge from chaos. Art was my outlet. It was always there to offer an escape.

After dressing, I placed a blank canvas on my easel and propped it by the window. I opened my art chest to reveal the many brushes and paints tucked inside. The anticipation was building. That night after dinner, I would harness all my fears. It was time to convey the sinking feeling in the pit of my stomach, for I expected the worst was yet to come.

✗ ✗ ✗

Adalynn's casserole was delicious. Comfort food was the perfect remedy. She even pulled out an expensive bottle of merlot. The warm, dark liquid unwound my tangled spirit and heated me pleasantly from the inside out. It was exactly what I needed. Even Miss King had a glass or two.

As we ate, I talked about my morning in downtown Willow Vale. Adalynn did not leave Kingsgrove—ever. The woman found comfort in her seclusion. All she had was Miss Peter's gossip to offer her a glimpse of the outside world. For the first time in a long time, she saw the world through another's eyes. In my own way, I told her about the Carmichaels and their little dog Boo-Radley. I even described Louanne and Hollis in their full glory, and shared a new-found desire to paint their portraits, curlers and all.

For some reason, I did not mention *The Eventide Emporium* and my run-in with Scarlet. The whole experience was so obscure, and to be honest, kind of a blur.

After three glasses of wine, my mood had significantly improved. I washed the dishes, excused myself for the night, and went up to my room. The anticipation grew as I rummaged through a jar of splayed paintbrushes. I sat in front of the easel, and started mixing colors on my pallet. The blank, white canvas faced me. It was empty and full of possibilities. When a numbing sense of calm came over me, I knew the stark surface was daring me to begin.

For many hours to follow, my hand seemed to have a mind of its own. It was unlike all the other paintings I had done before. That night, I was not in control. Every paint stroke came from a force separate from my own. I felt possessed, compelled, and fully con-sumed. The energy that surrounded me was exquisite. The sensation was familiar. The same static charge manifested as in my bed the other night, except this time it was different. I was not afraid. My mind and body were far too disconnected.

The possession continued on into the night. The sun set and was replaced by the moon. The moon rose, then set, and was replaced by the dawn. My neck ached and my hands were shaking as I applied the finishing touches. Once the final stroke of paint hit the canvas, the electric grip dissipated and left me completely. My eyes were dry and begging for rest, but I could not tear them away.

A young man in his twenties stood alone in the painting. A thick rolling fog surrounded him while moss-coated trees loomed in the background. His clothes were old fashioned and hung wet off his frame, as he stood, shin deep in the everglades. His dark, brown hair was damp and dishevelled. The man seemed to plead for help with arms reaching for my guidance. The most disturbing part was his eyes, or lack thereof. For in their place were two bright, white magnolias. They concealed most of his face, making the man impossible to recognize.

I had no idea what possessed me to paint such a thing. Purely out of fatigue, I simply blamed the wine.

My eyes began to droop, so I tidied my supplies and prepared for bed. I lay down and tried to sleep. The young man continued to beseech me from the dark picture across the room. It was haunting. I threw my sheets aside, crossed my room, and covered the painting with a scarf. Satisfied, I slid back under my sheets. The last thing I remembered was my head hitting the pillow.

✗ ✗ ✗

The next day was spent outside on the grounds with Adalynn. She peacefully roamed the garden, weeding out the undesirables. I, on the other hand, battled the heat while tackling some long-overdue yard work.

The sky brewed overhead as I cut the grass. One minute the yard was bright, and the next, it was dark. The old mower puttered and coughed as I stopped pushing to look up. My expectations of a wicked storm were assured by the thick, black clouds overhead. They rolled and swelled at an alarming rate. My skin tingled. The energy in the air was so tangible; it had me thoroughly on edge.

Once the grass was trim, I made my way to the river. The heat was relentless. It distorted the horizon in hazy waves, as if the air itself was melting. Feeling faint and desperate for relief, I dropped to my knees, which sank into the moist soil by the bank. Hands cupped, I gathered water and splashed my face, sending sweet chills down my spine. I took another handful to my hair and delighted in the sensation as water trailed down my sun-kissed chest.

For a while, I stayed hidden in the shade with my eyes closed, lashes heavy with cool droplets. Through the sound of my breathing, I could only hear the roar of rushing water. Soon, my thoughts drifted back to the eerie painting in my bedroom. That morning, I did not dare to lift the scarf. The young man in my dream was the same man with magnolias for eyes. This I knew, without a doubt.

But what did it all mean? Was it all just a product of my active imagination?

I opened my eyes and squinted against the bright assault of daylight. The sun had come out for a momentary tease. Sadly, the ominous sky still held a promise of bad weather to come. Before long, the clouds took over and the sun was lost again.

My fingers skimmed along the cool surface of the river. I reached deeper to find a few stones that were polished by the tumbling current. I tried to skip some unsuccessfully. It was a technique that I was never able to master.

On my quest for more rocks, something odd caught my eye. Imbedded in the riverbank was a bone colored object. I freed it from the ground and held it in the palm of my hand. It was an old pocketknife with a handle made of ivory. The blade was out and corroded with rust. Who knows how long it had been there. It was buried deep in the soil, blade first.

The knife was truly something special. At least it had been at one time. The handle was skilfully carved and inlayed with silver. I flipped it over and saw the initials M.K. engraved on the side. I assumed that the K stood for King. But whose name started with M?

I ran through all the members of the King family by memory: Jonathan, Evelyn, Violet, Alice, Tabitha Rose, Emma Rose, and Adalynn. There was no match that I knew of. M.K. was probably a relative, I decided and I started walking toward the house. All I wanted to do was clean the knife to see what was under all the mud and rust.

Soon after, I found myself standing over the kitchen sink with the pocketknife in one hand and a soapy scouring pad in the other. While deciding where to begin, I examined the strange object once again. To my surprise, the carved initials had vanished! I could not believe my eyes! I pushed the dirt around with my thumb in disbelief, but it was true. The two letters were gone!

How was it possible?

I stared at the knife for quite some time, searching for an answer. Eventually, I gave in, and started to scour the blade, ever so gently. The brown rust slowly lifted and rinsed away amidst the soapy water. With a careful hand, I managed to salvage most of the remaining steel. It was dull and the tip had rotted away, but in some parts, the blade still shone. Even though the pocketknife was damaged and imperfect, I began to form a strange attachment to it.

With a firm grip and a little canola oil, I was able to coax the blade back into the handle. I dried it thoroughly and held it up to the light. I was admiring my handiwork when Adalynn entered the room. She stopped dead in her tracks the moment she saw the knife in my hand.

"I found this on the riverbank. Someone must have dropped it in a long time ago. Do you recognize it Ada?" I said and offered it to her. She took the knife from my hand and examined it closely. Her eyes glistened with tears. My heart ached at the sight of her pain. "You must know who it belonged to," I said quietly. "Take it."

Miss King shook her head *no* and gave it back. She folded my hand tightly around the ivory handle. The gesture was final. Adalynn gave the mysterious knife to me. In that moment, I knew it was special gift.

Adalynn turned away and put the kettle on to boil. I took one last look at the knife, and slid it into my pocket. We spent the remainder of the afternoon together, sharing tea and lunch. After eating, Miss King gave me the *Willow Vale Gazette* to read out loud. I learned about an upcoming event called the *Backwater Summer*

Fair. It would begin one week from that day. The article listed off all the events and festivities. Adalynn did not appear the least bit interested. She looked past me with a vacant stare, and seemed a million miles away. I read on as she listlessly spun her empty teacup around in its saucer.

The *Backwater Summer Fair* sounded kind of fun, I thought. After all, my weekends were free, and it would give me something to do. Of course, I would be alone and surrounded by strangers, enjoying the festival with all their friends and family. It crossed my mind that the entire experience could be a miserable one. Then again, *it was summer* in Willow Vale. It was such a beautiful place, and the atmosphere alone would be worth it. *Carpe diem*, I told myself and decided to fully embrace my solitude once again. Miss King accepted her solitude with grace. She and I were more alike than I initially thought. We were an interesting pair—two lone wolves without a pack. Despite my mixed feelings about Kingsgrove, in that moment, I was happy to have found the unusual woman that lived here.

Both Adalynn and I were deep in thought when a ghostly whistle passed through the old estate. The wind had picked up and was fitfully thrashing the exterior of the house. The spooky sound was a forewarning that certainly had our attention. We looked each other dead in the eye.

"It's coming," I said to Miss King, and she nodded in agreement.

A deep rumble in the distance announced the approaching storm. I quickly made my way through the house, closing and latching all the shutters and windows. The boiling humidity had turned into an even damper drop in temperature. Already in the west wing, I went to my room to change. I slipped on an old pair of moccasins and a hooded sweatshirt to drive the chills away.

Without warning, a jagged crack of lightening hit a nearby tree. The sound was deafening. I jumped with fright as the house shook violently underfoot. With my tail between my legs, I hustled down the stairs to the main floor. Miss King was in the east parlor, cooped up on the loveseat. Daylight was fleeting, so all the lamps in the room and front foyer were turned on. Ada was placing two white candlesticks into matching silver holders just as I walked in.

Again, lightening split the evening sky and the parlor was suddenly bright with a brilliant flash. The crackling energy from the storm sent a shiver down my spine. I had never been in the middle of such a vicious storm. It was both intimidating *and* exciting.

Every muscle in my body was tense. I gripped the seat and braced myself for the next assault. Heaps of rain poured down and hammered on the roof above. A nearby clock ticked and echoed as if it were counting down . . . *tick-tock, tick-tock, tick-tock*. Time dragged on, increasing the anticipation.

Just as I began to loosen my grip, the moment came—*KAPOW!* The strike was so powerful that I jumped and squeezed my eyes shut. Every light bulb that was turned on blew up in succession. They popped, one after the other, sending shards of thin glass into the air. I screamed out of shock, and then the room was coated in darkness.

Adalynn did not make a sound.

My eyes widened like a startled cat's in attempt to penetrate the pitch-black. Just as the panic began to set in, I heard the strike of a match. Adalynn appeared in the flame. The fiery, amber light distorted her face, giving the woman a fierce and menacing expression. She lit both candles and handed me one of the silver holders. I placed my finger through the ring and rested the base on my lap.

With a shaky voice, I said, "You probably have some blown fuses. It used to happen at my grandmother's house, so I know how to replace them. Can you show me where to find the fuse box? I should change them before we go to bed." Ada stood up and led me by candlelight into the foyer. She took me down a narrow corridor, behind the grand staircase.

It felt as if someone was watching as we walked through the darkness. The atmosphere seemed to change with every thunderbolt that tore across the sky. I could have sworn the sounds of disembodied footsteps were stalking me. Nerves tingling, I turned swiftly to investigate. I held my candle out, but saw nothing. Our only pursuers were the morphing shadows behind me.

My skin crawled and chills spread through my body in perpetual waves. I turned back and could no longer see the glow from Adalynn's candle. How did she leave me so quickly? My heart dropped to the floor. I was suddenly alone with only a meager flame to guide me.

Hoping she was just up ahead, I followed the dark corridor, and only found a dead-end.

A dead-end?

Where was Miss King? There was nowhere for her to go!

Panic was crushing me in its icy grip. I reached the end of the hall, and felt some sweet relief, as it actually turned a corner to the right. The prowling shadows had deceived me. I went around the bend and stopped abruptly in shock. If not for the sight of her flame, I would have collided brutally with Adalynn. She was waiting in silence by a closed door.

Miss King unhooked the latch and pushed open the stiff door. The screech of its hinges resonated throughout the narrow passage. She gestured for me to go in, and I stood before the entrance. Looking up at me was the basement of Kingsgrove.

No, not the basement! I was hoping the fuse box was on the main floor, stuffed in a closet somewhere.

What had I gotten myself into now?

I wanted to tell her, *not a chance* and turn on my heels, but then remembered it was my job. I had given my word. After all, we could not spend the whole night in darkness. At least I couldn't—not in that house. No way!

The rumble of thunder mingled with the sound of my pounding heart. I looked down into a pit of pure black. The dusty staircase was lost in the gloom. There was nothing welcoming about the dark underbelly of the century-old home. My imagination ran wild, and even though my intuition cried out against it, I forced myself to take the first step.

My nose twitched as I breathed the musty air from the dank room below. Here goes nothing, I thought to myself, and concealed the burning candle with a protective hand. *Please stay lit, please stay lit, please stay lit.* I repeated the mantra over and over in my mind. The fear was intoxicating, and the silver holder shook perilously in my hand. My destroyed nerves were turning my own body against me. The dancing flame was my only lifeline.

It *had* to stay lit.

The wooden steps creaked with every footfall. I reached the bottom of the stairs and the foul sensation of cobwebs coated my face and mouth. I spat them from my lips and rubbed the rest off on my sleeve. Feeling vulnerable, I pulled the hood of my sweater up over my head.

The light from the candle leapt up the walls. It lurked and formed around the dusty beams and pipes. I would have given anything in that moment to have a proper flashlight. Why was Miss King so archaic in her ways?

Using the candle, I scanned the walls for a fuse box. Through the muffled sound of the storm, I started to hear whispering. It was in front of me, behind me, all around me, and in my head. I was about to make a run for it when I saw a row of metal boxes.

I quickly went to work and turned off the main power. The labels were stained yellow and faded, making them impossible to read. With trembling hands, I removed all the fuses that were clearly blown. Luckily, there were a few new ones stored on a shelf nearby. I took a box, dropped it, and the fuses scattered. I frantically clawed at the ground to find them. It was awful. The whispers taunted me. I struggled to keep it together, but fumbled pathetically and uncontrollably with fear.

Somehow, I managed to screw in all the matching fuses with the correct amperage. At least, I hoped it was right. There was only one way to know for sure. I held my breath, and flipped on the main switch. The sound of surging electricity followed, and the power was restored!

A quivering exhale fell from my lips. The whispering was starting to get louder. Whimpering with fright, I spun around to look for a switch for the basement light. What I found instead was the biggest shock of my life.

I was standing, face to face . . . with a ghost!

It was an apparition of a young man. His tousled hair was dark compared to his skin, which was pale and transparent like white gossamer. He had a striking face that was twisted in anguish. His teeth were bared and his hazel eyes blazed with a manic intensity. He grabbed hold of my shoulders. His grip sent a fierce, electrical charge through my body. In a strangled voice, the ghost whispered two words that I would never forget.

"Free . . . Me . . ."

I screamed louder than ever before. The candle flew from my hand and went out as it hit the ground. On hands and knees, I crawled frantically across the stone-cold floor. By some miracle, I found the bottom of the staircase and climbed out of the basement. My skin was slashed and torn from stumbling painfully up every step.

The darkness was everywhere.

All I saw was black!

I ran blindly down the hallway and used outstretched hands to feel for the wall. Straight away, I tripped on something and landed hard. The fall knocked the wind right out of me and the carpet skinned my knees raw. Adrenaline pumped ferociously through my body. The rush fueled me. It lifted me up and pulled me, staggering out into the foyer. All I wanted was my car keys and to get the hell out of that house. But Miss King was blocking the front door! The flame of her candle formed a mask of harsh shadows on her face. In my crazed state, I saw the woman only as my enemy. She was holding me hostage in a horrific place.

I acted on instinct alone. "I'm sorry Ada! I have to go! I can't stay here!" I explained manically while reaching desperately for my keys. She held her free hand out in a feeble attempt to stop me. I averted her easily and rushed out the door.

My moccasins were lost somewhere along the way. I hadn't even realized until my bare feet hit the muddy ground running. The rain still poured, soaking me in an instant. With a slip and another near fall, I flung the car door open and threw myself in the driver's seat. My haggard breathing was filled with hysteria and my motor skills were weak and frantic. After dropping my key twice on the floor of the car, I finally pushed it into the ignition and started the engine.

I would not feel safe until Willow Vale disappeared from my rear-view mirror.

As I sped down Kings Lane, leaving the haunted grove behind, all I saw was that face—that white, ghostly face. Those hazel eyes were seared directly to my soul.

THE GHOST

The rain was relentless, hindering my already difficult getaway. A tempest of wind and water battered the vehicle as I relied on my high beams as the only guiding light. Kings Lane was a mess of soggy ruts and deep puddles. I regretted leaving my shoes behind as my bare foot worked the gas pedal. In fact, I left more behind than just my shoes. I left my clothes, my art . . . my home. I had nothing. Sadness washed over me like the pouring rain on my windshield.

No matter what was left behind, there was no going back. I had seen a ghost! It reached out and grabbed me! My mind was still reeling from the shocking encounter. I pressed my foot down on the gas pedal and sped through the mud. There was no going back, I told myself again. Kingsgrove was haunted!

Lightning struck once more, sending a tremor of thunder in its wake. I gripped the wheel and scrunched down into my shoulders. My body trembled with the blow. Seeing the ghost was my undoing. Everything I thought I knew had altered. There was so much more to *life and death* than I ever thought possible. The instinct to run battled with my conflicted heart.

Was I really going to leave Willow Vale and never look back? Where would I go?

Another realization came crashing down like thunder. I had forgotten about Adalynn. I casted her aside and left without even saying goodbye. The strange and silent woman had had an unexpected effect on me. Although we were moving toward friendship, there was something unusual about her behavior that night.

Why did she try to stop me from leaving? It was as if she had anticipated the moment. For some reason, Miss King knew I was going to make a run for it.

Did she expect the young man to appear? It was hard to believe, but there was no other explanation. When I went down into the basement, she headed for the door. Miss King was prepared to stop me in case I tried to leave. I wondered why, then remembered Adalynn had spent a lifetime hidden away in that house. She *had* to know it was haunted.

My mind was so engaged that I nearly drove down into a deep pool of murky water. The road in front of me had completely washed out. My spirit plummeted as the car idled on the edge of the blockade. There was nothing left to do but press my forehead to the steering wheel and cry. All the pent-up anxiety was released with every sob. The ghost's face troubled me the most. It was so scary and so tormented.

Those eyes! They tore at my soul and begged for release.

In time, the heavy tears subsided and I just sat there, letting them dry on my cheeks. Eventually, I felt better. The pieces began to mend. I wiped my face with a damp sleeve, and took some deep soothing breaths. Instead of running on impulse, I took a moment to reflect.

My thoughts were so jumbled that I began with the most obvious question—who was the young man? He had been trying to reach me since the moment I arrived in Willow Vale. The whispers, the phantom footsteps, the painting . . . the nightmares—the ghost was behind it all.

I remembered the young man's desperate plea, *Free . . . Me . . .*

Free him from what?

When he grabbed me, I could feel the energy flow between us. It had become a familiar sensation. I had felt him before. *He* was the one in my bed that night. I touched my cheek. It tingled with the memory.

Was he really out to get me? Was I really in danger?

Now that my mind was clear, I realized that the ghost needed my help. Somehow, I could see and feel his spirit. In some way, he thought I could set him free.

Kingsgrove was absolutely terrifying and full of dark secrets. I did not know how to help the ghost, but I could try. There had to be a way to overpower my fears and return to Kingsgrove. Before changing my mind, I grabbed the steering wheel and carefully turned the car around.

✗ ✗ ✗

The sound of a classical melody echoed beautifully throughout Kingsgrove. The storm had passed, and there I stood in the foyer, barefoot and soaking wet. The lamps were lit, and the home felt calm and warm. Reluctantly, I peeked through the double doors into the parlor. Ada was knitting quietly on the window seat. When I entered, she did not look up. Instead, she pointed to a white towel, folded in front of her. I took the towel and gratefully buried myself in it. The thick terrycloth was soft and smelled of lilacs.

Miss King looked so peaceful in that moment. I approached slowly and placed a tentative hand on her shoulder. She took her own hand and rested it gently on mine. Nothing needed to be said. I was sorry for running away. She was glad I came back. Words were not necessary.

I left the parlor then made my way to the servant's quarters. Slowly, I ascended the steps. My muscles ached and burned. I was grateful the lights were working again, for all my anxiety had returned. However, instead of running, I was going to do the opposite. I was going to confront the ghost that haunted Kingsgrove.

In the privacy of my bedroom, I peeled off my wet sweatshirt and shorts. While undressing, I felt vulnerable and exposed. Was someone watching me—someone I could not see? I grabbed the towel and wrapped my naked body tightly inside. The possibility that I was not alone was unnerving, to say the least.

I turned on the washroom light, and saw that my legs were in bad shape. They were muddy, bruised, scratched, and streaked with dried blood. I ran some warm water and carefully cleaned my wounds. The dirt and blood merged and slipped down the drain. Once the water ran clear, I slowly lifted myself from the tub and grabbed a fresh towel. Methodically, I dried my tender body and dressed in a cotton t-shirt and pyjama shorts. I crawled onto the bed and sat cross-legged in the center.

"Here I am," I called out to the empty room. There was no reply. "I'm done running. I ran away before and ended up here. I tried to run away tonight, and here I am again. That must mean something, right?" My eyes blurred with tears. "You asked me for something tonight. If you need my help, I'm here now. Ask away."

The room remained silent. I sat patiently, waiting as time passed. Sleep was not an option, whether the ghost showed itself or not. I was prepared to wait all night.

For a while, nothing happened. Then, slowly, a sequence of strange things began to transpire. The ticking clock on the dresser suddenly stopped. All sounds were sucked away, and the energy in the room pulsated. My arms prickled with goose bumps, and my cheeks flushed with anticipation and fear. I closed my eyes and could feel the weight of someone sitting on the bed before me.

Terror seized my body. It had come! The ghost was in front of me!

My breath shuddered and caught in my throat. I bit my lips to suppress the fear then slowly opened one eye at a time, and there he was. I jumped back on the bed, out of reflex. My heart pounded as I stared in disbelief.

There were no glowing orbs or black smoke. He was more like a faded imprint, or a dim projection of a man from the past. The apparition flickered in and out of sight, and his movements were strained and broken.

I was completely awestruck at the sight of him. Although his dark hair and old-fashioned clothes were in disarray, the young man was stunning. He had a face that could haunt me for this life and the next.

"Who are you?" My voice was quiet and unsteady.

His lips parted, but as he tried to speak, his image dissolved and nearly disappeared. I panicked and reached for his hands. As we made contact, a vibrant, electric charge overcame me. I felt it permeate my entire body. The ghost's image brightened instantly. He looked down in amazement at the unexpected embrace.

As we absorbed the powerful connection between us, our eyes met. His were wide and fierce. The young man spoke, and his voice was full of wonder. "Remarkable girl. You can see me?"

I nodded.

"Will you free me, Emilie?" His anguish returned.

"How?" I had no idea where to start. "I don't even know who you are."

"I can't say." Sounding weaker, he struggled with the words.

"I don't know what you mean." I felt tired and so confused.

He looked down, and his face filled with sorrow. "You're hurt." He freed one hand and traced a finger over a cut on my leg. The ghostly touch gave me a new rush of chills.

My cheeks burned red. "I'm fine. It's nothing."

The ghost's hand lingered on my knee. I was mesmerized by the sensation. In time, he lifted his gaze to meet my own. "Will you help me, Emilie?"

"Yes." My response was simple, and easier said than done.

"You need to look around you. All the answers are there." He saw my puzzled expression. "I will help guide you. It's all I can do." He started to fade again. "You can win this. The darkest hour of night could not overpower you. I can see your spirit . . . it is luminescent." He touched my pale hair and then the bird on my locket. As if trying to unearth some distant memory, the ghost stared at the necklace. His intensity soon turned into a look of realization. With tired eyes, he looked up at me in reverence. "It's you! You're the white hawk . . ."

I was too drained to make sense of his words. All my energy was passed to the ghost so he could stay. Alas, there was nothing left. In our final moment of strength, we gazed into each other's eyes— blue and hazel. The last thing I remembered was his phantom arms around me. He lowered me to the bed and quietly slipped away.

X X X

I was torn from a deep sleep by the vulgar cry of a raven. The intruder was perched on my windowsill and aggressively flapping its wings. I threw my sheets aside, and crossed the room to shoo the bird away. It launched into an attack, clawing and pecking as I approached. My eyes scanned the room and found the scarf draped over my painting. I grabbed it, and swiftly wrapped the material around my arm. Using it as a defence, I managed to fend off the bird and close the window. The raven continued to thrash up against the glass. My adrenaline pumped until the animal relinquished and flew away. I could hardly believe the unusual and unprovoked attack.

I raked my hands through my hair and remembered the window being closed the night before. Then another tidal wave of memories came flooding back. After all, how does one forget a rendezvous with a ghost?

The scarf fell silently to the floor as I turned to face the painting. It was unveiled, and the haunting image beseeched me once again. Although I was overwhelmed and mystified by its significance, one thing had changed indefinitely. The painting no longer scared me. Instead, all I saw was a canvas stained with heartache.

My fingertips grazed over the painted surface and rested on the man's shrouded face. Seeing the mask of white magnolias gave me a sudden revelation. I sailed across the room and searched frantically through a basket of my dirty clothes. The denim shorts I needed were at the very bottom. There was a small piece of notepaper in the back pocket. Lying between the folds was a pair of sad eyes. A few days had passed since I drew the picture in Mr. King's office. I held it for a second time, and saw more than simple pencil sketch. I placed the sad eyes over the magnolias, and the young man's face was complete. The cryptic message was clear. He had been trying to reveal himself all along. I looked fondly at the painted stranger. We were truly connected in some unearthly way.

"I wish I knew your name," I spoke quietly. "What happened to you? Why do you feel so trapped?" When there was no reply, I sat despairingly on the edge of the bed. "What do I have to do?" I touched the hawk on my silver locket, and took a deep breath. Even though it was a hopeless situation, the ghost needed me. I could not resist his desperate plea for help. The mysterious quest had me spellbound.

The bizarre encounter with the raven was soon forgotten; my thoughts were too preoccupied. It was the weekend, which gave me two solid days of freedom. It was time to explore Willow Vale and find some answers. I expected that a little willpower and a lot of research would point me in the right direction. With a simple plan in place, I was ready to start the day.

After getting dressed, I grabbed my messenger bag and headed to the kitchen. Through the doorway, I saw JoJo Peters pass Adalynn a bottle of prescription pills. The nurse spoke quietly and gestured to a pamphlet on the counter. Adalynn saw me standing in the entrance and quickly hid everything under a dishtowel.

"Sorry. I'm intruding." I turned to leave.

"Heavens no! We're all set. Aren't we, Adalynn?" JoJo persisted. Miss King nodded, poured some tea, and handed me a cup. The essence of Earl Grey wafted in my face as I took a little sip.

"Quite the storm we had last night, wasn't it dear?" JoJo said to me. "Shoulda seen the pit of water I drove through this mornin'! I was 'bout to go fetch a dingy and come back." She smiled and her eyes wrinkled at the corners. "So how did ya'll make out here last night?"

"Umm. It was fine. We lit candles and played cards until the storm passed." I shot a brief glance at Adalynn as I lied. The woman did not even flinch.

"Glad to hear it. So what's your plan for the weekend?" JoJo asked and held out a tray of muffins. "Made these myself."

"Thanks!" I took one gratefully and peeled off the paper liner. "I'm going to stop by the library, and then do some exploring."

"That's nice dear." The nurse smiled wide and turned her attention back to Adalynn.

I ate my muffin while listening to JoJo's detailed rendition of the latest local scandal. As the story ended, I wished the ladies a good day and went out into the foyer. After strapping on my sandals, I lingered for a moment in the doorway. "I'll be back soon." My private message was just barely a whisper.

To my surprise, there was a faint response. "I'll be waiting." I could feel his cool breath on the back of my neck. The sensation that followed was altogether thrilling. He was right behind me, and for some reason, I could not stop myself from smiling.

SECRETS OF EDEN

The *Willow Vale Public Library* towered over me. The looming structure was a shining example of an old-world academic institution. In other words, it was kind of intimidating. The task I was about to embark on was a little out of my comfort zone. Sure, I had read a few novels in my time, but that was different. Devouring a dog-eared page-turner over a latte was nothing like digging up and decoding old documents and records. The mind-numbing, technical side of life stressed me out. Artistic pursuits were always more attractive. Lead and paper, paint and canvas, these were the things I understood the most. Apart from that, I was more of a *used bookstore* kind of girl. While in school, I rarely wandered the library stacks along with the other studious bookworms. On one occasion, during freshman year, I had gotten seriously lost while searching for the campus art studio. It was afterhours and every empty hallway looked like the last. Before I knew it, I was trapped in a vast labyrinth of texts and paperbacks.

The library in Willow Vale was not your average study hall. The old building was large and imposing—a fortress of stained glass and stone. I pushed open the heavy doors and stood in the lobby like a lost puppy. Surrounding me was a marble oasis, ruled by a dainty brunette. The young woman had skin like caramel. She wore a braided scarf around her mass of dark curls, and her nymph-like face was hidden behind a pair of oversized glasses. They slipped down her nose as she leaned over the colossal desk to greet me. "*Bonjour cherie.* Can I help you?" The librarian spoke in a hushed Creole accent.

"Actually, yes. That would be great." I mimicked her quiet tone. "I would like to do some research on an estate that I just moved into. Have you heard of Kingsgrove?"

"*C'est vrai?* You must be that *Wyld* girl that moved in with Miss King." Her golden eyes widened at the realization. "*Manman,* my mother, spoke of this last week with the women from her sewing circle. It's a pleasure to meet you in person. I'm Ruby Monrose."

The small-town busybodies had struck again.

"Emilie Wyld." I returned the introduction. Not that it mattered.

"Come Emilie. I will help." The librarian got up from her desk then hopped off the platform it sat on. I was instantly surprised at how petit she was. Compared to me, Ruby Monrose was pintsized.

I sat at a table and watched as she darted in and out of the isles like a squirrel gathering its nuts. A stack of her findings was promptly placed before me. "There, I think this'll do," she whispered and laid the final book on the pile.

"Thanks," I said, bewildered. Ruby must have sensed my anxiety, for she hesitated to leave. "I'll be okay from here," I assured her. "You've been a massive help." She smiled warmly then headed back to her desk.

I watched Ruby walk away, and snickered at the irony of her occupation. She was such a tiny librarian in charge of all those books—a guardian of literature and history, so vigilant, yet sweet and unassuming.

I rifled through the mountain of research and sighed. Thankfully, Ruby Monrose was there to help. It would have been impossible to find all that material without her. There was everything from plat books, deeds, and property guides to township directories and filed newspaper clippings.

My morning venture quickly became a frenzy of page flipping and chaotic note taking. In time, I went over my scribbles and saw a vague story begin to unravel.

Kingsgrove was built in 1895. In 1921, Evelyn and Jonathan King were married. They inherited the estate and paper mill, soon after. Mr. King ran the mill lucratively until he died from a heart attack in 1959. He was sixty-two years old. Without a male heir to take over, the mill was sold, and then eventually closed down in 1983. Shortly after her husband's passing, Evelyn had a stroke and died in her sleep. All the daughters, excluding Adalynn, were married then widowed. None of them had children, just as JoJo said.

Within the countless newspaper clippings, I found a few significant obituaries and articles. The brittle papers revealed that Adalynn's sisters had all passed away within the last twenty years. The most recent one died only four years before, due to complications from pneumonia. All of the King woman were brought back to Kingsgrove and laid to rest in the cemetery. Violet's obituary affirmed that her family was very fond of the property, and of one another.

While reading, I kept an eye open for the initials M.K., and found nothing. The knife was in the pocket of my jeans. I could feel the ivory handle press against my thigh. Even though the old relic was practically useless, I liked knowing it was there. Despite its flaws, the knife made me feel safe.

My stomach growled, and I looked up at the clock. It was already past noon. The minutes were ticking by, and my patience was wearing thin. Not a single word, in all those papers and books, even suggested who haunted Kingsgrove. Who could he be? Out of frustration, I rested my head down on my folded arms. The library was my only hope. I needed just one little breadcrumb to coax me in the right direction—just one.

Out of nowhere, a slight draft passed through and flipped a page over in the plat book. I lifted my head and looked around. There were no open windows, and the sudden breeze had already died off.

I looked over at the plat book and pulled it in close. The page had flipped from The Kingsgrove Estate to another land map in Willow Vale. The plot was small, and located about a mile and a half from Kingsgrove. It sat deep in the woods with no main-road access.

I pushed aside the plat book, grabbed the property guide, and flicked through the pages. Interestingly enough, the records showed that an old cabin was built on the property. I delved back into the pile of documents, and before long, the deed was in my hand. I saw the owner's name, and my jaw dropped.

What a twist of fate! The land belonged to Scarlet Eventide.

I went over the documents again, and it appeared that Scarlet had inherited the small home and property from her guardian and grandmother, Olivia. With vigor, I searched through the newspaper clippings and found one article on a woman named Dyana Eventide. It was written that she died in her mother's home during childbirth in 1958. Olivia was the woman's mother. That meant Scarlet Eventide was the baby. The details of Dyana's sad end were completely glossed over. I looked for more excerpts on the three women with no success. There was no record of Olivia Eventide's death, or any mention of husbands or fathers either. It seemed that we had more in common than I had initially thought.

Perhaps the Eventides enjoyed their privacy, and did not like to share all the finer details of their lives. They did practice Voodoo, after all. I imagined all the God-fearing locals clutching their Bibles whenever someone spoke the name *Eventide*. Scarlet and her emporium of oddities definitely stood out in sleepy town of Willow Vale. I was sure she had few righteous people praying for her soul.

I sat back in my chair, and a murky blend of dates and names swam around in my head. Even though I did not know what to make of Scarlet, the fact that she owned a property so close to Kingsgrove *was* interesting. I wondered if a footpath from the estate to her hidden cabin in the woods existed. If it did, I was definitely going to find it.

I got up and tidied the books on the table. After my notes were stuffed inside my bag, I went to see Ruby at her desk. She was deeply absorbed in a thick, old book. Her glasses were still perched on the tip of her nose.

I cleared my throat. She jumped at the sound, and then a smile spread across her face. "How did you do, *cherie*?"

"Very well, thanks to you," I said in all honesty, and then asked, "Do you know where I could find a trail map or back road guide of Willow Vale?"

Ruby began to search through the many drawers in her large desk. That was when I noticed the necklace dangling from her neck. The chain held an octagon pendant made of silver. It had an emblem of eight spears in a starburst pattern. "*Bon*. I knew I'd seen these here before." She reached out to hand me a map booklet. Her tiny wrist rattled with a bracelet made of beads and cowry shells. The style of her jewelry looked familiar, though I did not know why.

"This should take you where you need to go," she said sweetly as I took the booklet from her hand.

"Thanks again." I waved goodbye and turned to leave.

"Emilie!" Ruby raised her voice to stop me. She glanced around in fear of disturbing the other library patrons. I came closer, and she spoke intently. "If there is anything else you need help with, please come back. I'm always here to lend a hand." I sensed the uneasiness in her tone. "Ba bye, Miss Wyld. And *bonne chance*."

I held up the booklet in a gesture of appreciation, and left the library. Ruby's kindness seemed authentic. She was endearing from head-to-toe. I liked her.

The moment the library doors were open, I was accosted by the heat. The sunny day was perfect for a walk, so I set out on a pursuit to appease my hunger. There were vibrant banners everywhere to advertise for the upcoming *Backwater Summer Fair*. Using my hands to shade my eyes, I watched as the banners flapped freely in the wind.

A small restaurant came into view as I walked up the street. The sign read, *Kitty's Catfish Diner*. I entered and sat down in a quiet booth. The smell of Cajun cuisine was mouth-watering. When the waitress came over, I ordered a bowl of seafood gumbo and a tall glass of sweet tea.

As I ate, my thoughts began to drift. Once there was a moment to reflect, I could not help but feel totally wonderstruck. Willow Vale was a strange place that was altogether magical. In such a short time, my whole world had become tangled up and twisted. I ran away from the past, and had fallen deep into a hollow of mystery. I had fallen down the rabbit hole.

Feeling like my mouth was on fire, I pushed the spicy bowl of gumbo aside and drank some sweet tea to cool my heated lips. The trail book was open on the table in front of me. I flipped through the pages and saw that every river and swimming hole was clearly marked and labelled. Swimming was my favorite thing to do, besides drawing and painting.

Using a finger, I followed the river that ran behind the Kingsgrove Estate. Not too far along was the perfect spot for a private swim. The river branched off to a small body of water named Willowmere Lake. There was a trail off Kings Lane that led right to it. I tapped the tiny, blue paper lake with a fingertip. It was time to do something for myself and clear my weary mind. Before diving into a pit of chaos, I was going to dive into Willowmere Lake.

✗ ✗ ✗

With the map book in hand, I drove slowly down Kings Lane in search of the trails opening. Finally, an unkempt path was exposed. I was relieved to see a makeshift, wooden sign nailed to a tree trunk in the aperture. The name of the lake was carved into the sun-bleached plank of wood. I parked the Trans Am along the edge of the narrow road and got out.

The trail was a little muddy, though some areas were already dry from the baking sun. Ribbons of light shone down on the forest floor, guiding me along the winding path. While the dense canopy and Spanish moss provided some shade, it was still stiflingly hot. I longed for shorts instead of jeans, but my legs were battered and bruised. To avoid a new wave of rumors about the blonde girl from the north, I chose to cover up.

Thankfully, the lake was not too far from Kings Lane. Soon enough, Willowmere came into view, and it was nothing short of breathtaking. I took a moment to enjoy the scene set before me.

The water was clear and alive, glistening with sunlight. It was as if rhinestones had fallen from the sky and were gliding over the pleated surface. Monstrous trees stood anchored by their twisted bottoms. I was surrounded by a myriad of green. It crawled and crept over every rock and root. I closed my eyes and listened. The birds were singing a chorus of unique harmonies. It was my own private concert of delightful twitters and trills.

Elated, I could not strip free of my clothing fast enough. The sun shone on my exposed skin. I hung my things on a tree branch and gingerly stepped onto a weathered dock. The wood was warm and soft on the soles of my feet. While naked and anxious on the edge, I dipped a toe in to test the water. It was sublime, and without another thought, I sprung from the dock and vanished beneath the surface. The contrast of hot and cold was both shocking and invigorating. My body plummeted into the deep basin. Once my descent slowed, I began to swim up toward the rippling light. I broke free and filled my lungs with delicious, fresh air. Exhilaration permeated my entire being.

I straightened up and lay on my back to float, allowing my ears fill and deafen. All I could hear was the sound of my steady breathing. It resounded in my head. The hot sun on my face and the cool water on my body quelled my restless spirit. I drifted around and basked in the secluded paradise. It was my Eden—my Shangri-La.

The lake was like a peaceful mirage, allowing all my troubles to slip away. My guard was down, and for the first time in Willow Vale, I felt completely at ease. I thought Willowmere was a safe place where I could be alone . . . until . . . cold fingers dragged along my open palm.

In an instant, those fingers locked around my hand. I thrashed around and wrenched my body to see who was there. When I saw the perpetrator, my heart stopped. It was the ghost! The young man was in the lake with me.

Gasping for breath, I tried to hide myself underwater while treading vulnerably before him.

"You scared me!" I accused the ghost, heart thumping in my chest.

"You're here. I found you." His smile was wide, and his eyes gleamed in the sunlight. His image was sheer and fluid, much like the water that surrounded us.

"I'm naked!" I declared in horror. The ghost did not seem to notice. He was clothed in his 1940s attire and regarded me with that same look of wonder. He was across from me, chest deep in the water. It was arcane and unnatural to see him floating there like that. The water barely moved around him. "How are you here?" I choked back the fear and asked.

"It's the water, Emilie. The water has the energy I need to come to you. You are the only one who can see. I have tried to see, and to be seen, so many times. For so many years I tried . . . and nothing." He drifted off. His face fell and filled with misery.

Being in the presence of a ghost was chilling; still, my heart broke for him. There were so many questions to ask, but the words refused to come. Instead, all I wanted was to ease his pain. *But how*, I wondered.

The ghost's image wavered, blinking in and out of sight. His face, softened with misery, revealed what was left of the broken boy still inside. Then, like a spark of light in my mind, déjà-vu took me by surprise. All the carefree summer days spent swimming with childhood friends came rushing back. A smirk curled at the corner of my mouth. With a flick of the hand, I splashed the surface, making in rain over the young man's face. He lifted his head, phantom-eyes wide in shock. The fearsome idea of swimming with a ghost vanished at the sight of his expression. Even a giggle escaped my lips.

Just as I hoped, his smile returned. It was stunning.

"Your laughter is ethereal. It's been so long since I've heard anything like it." In an instant, his smile turned into a whimsical and mischievous grin. He looked so young and impressive. "I have to hear it again," he declared then splashed me in return.

I laughed, swimming away from the playful assault. My checks burned from the grin radiating on my face. Not a moment later, I turned back around, still giggling.

The water settled around me. In a single breath, my happiness turned into confusion.

The ghost had disappeared.

I swam in a circle, surveying the lake around me. So quickly, he was there and then gone again. A pain blossomed in my heart—a hollow sort of pain that left me feeling empty once more. The ghost was gone, leaving me alone in the water, alone in my Eden— my Shangri-La.

DARK POISON

While rocking back and forth, my mind mimicked the same swaying motion. It was Sunday evening, and I was sitting on the porch swing at Kingsgrove. I loosely braided my ashen hair to satisfy my restless spirit. The braid fell and unravelled as I stood to lean over the porch railing. My eyes searched the endless blue sky, as if it held all the answers. Dusk was approaching and the sun was about to begin its journey toward the horizon. I had spent the entire weekend rewriting and rethinking all my messy notes and seemingly useless theories. Instead of making sense if it all, my thoughts only spiralled into a more deeply confused state. The little I knew hardly helped. I knew that all the members of the King family were dead, except for one. As strange as it was, there were no descendants. Without a single living relative, Adalynn was all that remained. As a result, the Kingsgrove Estate would likely be sold once her life ended. It was a shame considering the mill owner and his beautiful family loved the property so much. It was their home—it was a home built for a King.

To my knowledge, Jonathan was an honest businessman, and his success was earned with integrity. Ada's father lived up to his name, and was truly a king among men. His wife Evelyn and their daughters were the belles of Willow Vale. The women were respected for their kindness and admired for their sophisticated beauty.

Even though the history of Kingsgrove was glamorous, it was fairly uneventful. Other than Adalynn's brush with death, nothing momentous had happened. Based on that premise alone, I was left confused. With such a fortunate past, why was the estate haunted? There had been no murders or crimes committed on the property. There were no dark tragedies or unsolved mysteries linked to the area. Most importantly, there was no record of the young man ever living or dying there.

The ultimate question remained—who was the ghost?

Since the 1920s, the only man that lived at Kingsgrove was Jonathan. There were pictures of Mr. King, young and old, all throughout the house. The ghost had some similarities, but he lacked a few distinct characteristics. Along with that, the years did not correlate. In the 1940s, most young men were fighting overseas in World War II. The ghost looked like he belonged in that era. Everything about him was old-fashioned and charmingly vintage. Was the ghost a reflection of himself at the moment of his death? If so, then the young man likely died when Jonathan was still in his forties. I was convinced that Adalynn's father was not the young man I was seeing.

I had examined every piece of the puzzle scattered before me, aside from one. Thankfully, there was still one curious detail left unexplored. I did not see the connection between the Eventides and the ghost, but it *was* my only lead. My intuition cried out when the plat book flipped, oh so mysteriously, to display Scarlet's property. I knew then that it was not a coincidence. After all, the ghost did say that he would guide me. There was something that he wanted me to see, and that something was deep in the backwoods of Willow Vale. In hopes of finding another option, I had been avoiding the true task at hand—the ghost wanted me to find that cabin.

On the evening of the storm, the ghost had said, *You can win this.* He called me the white hawk. What did that even mean? I touched my locket and looked down at the silver pendent. I felt just as small as the tiny bird under my thumb.

I had not seen the ghost since we swam in Willowmere Lake the day before. It left me feeling lost and alone while trying to solve a hopeless riddle. On top of everything else, I found myself in another impossible situation. The way I felt was more frightening than any haunted house could be. The truth was, I missed him. It was senseless and completely ridiculous, but my heart had ignored all common sense. My stomach was in knots just thinking about it. I raked my hands through my hair and sighed.

What was happening to me?

I looked up to the sky again. Vibrant colors had stained the clouds overhead, marking the hour of sunset. The cabin was only a mile and a half from Kingsgrove. There was no time to lose. A race against the imminent approach of nightfall was upon me. Waiting for daybreak was the wiser choice, one could argue, though nothing could have stopped me at that moment. Without delay, I gathered up a few useful things to take along for the trip. I was a crazy girl, about to go on a crazy evening journey to a Voodoo cabin in the woods. I would need all the help I could get.

✗ ✗ ✗

I stood on the edge of the estate with the King family cemetery at my back. The gateway to the woods was an old bridge made of timber. The small handrails were my only barrier from the rushing river below. I turned around and looked up at the grand stone angels. They were vigilant in their eternal vocation to Mr. and Mrs. King. The two winged guardians showed such strength and devotion. I displayed my own sense of reckless devotion, with a map in one hand and an oil lantern in the other. Finding Scarlet's little cabin would be easy enough, I thought. Just follow the trail. It was a simple plan.

Without a second thought, I crossed over the bridge, entered the woods, and left the cemetery behind.

The thick underbrush clawed at my ankles as I hiked through the overgrown trail. The route had been forgotten and was buried in ferns. Fortunately, the scattered trees allowed enough daylight through to guide the way. The cypress trunks split the sun into beams of golden light. The rays hung dangerously low to the ground. Nevertheless, I was determined to reach the cabin before sunset. I could not sit back and wait for the answers to fall in my lap. The ghost needed me. For whatever reason, it was my quest to free him. I had to walk the path—I had to see it through.

As every minute passed, the forest faded to the dusk. Despite my stubborn conviction, the night was closing in. Everything that was green had already turned a drab shade of grey. In the depleting light, the forest had become a gothic land with a dark promise. My confidence had misled me. It was a mistake to enter the woods at nightfall, but it was too late to go back. According to the map, the cabin was close. I ignored the brewing anxiety and pressed on.

The forest was too quiet. The unnerving silence only broke when my sneakers hit the ground. That was, until I heard a peal of chimes ring in the distance. The eerie sound echoed through the air. Before long, I saw something unusual in the trees around me. There was an assembly of bizarre items hanging amongst the Spanish moss. There were bones, feathers, and little pouches strung up with twine. Each item was colorfully decorated with seashells and beads of glass. To get a closer look, I stopped to touch one of the exotic artefacts. I got distracted, and the item fell away from my hand. A rush of chills tingled down my spine when I saw how the shadows had grown. Every last ray of daylight was gone. The sun was set and a full moon, whole and bright, had risen in its place.

I kneeled down in the path and lit my lantern with a match. It instantly embraced me with a warm glow of yellow light. My anxiety passed for a moment, but as I stood up the world tilted. I braced myself against a nearby tree. The strange trinkets were everywhere. I could feel them brush against my face and tangle in my hair. The chimes rang in my ears and resonated in my head.

The dizzy spell was nauseating. My stomach retched and stars blinded my vision. As I fought the sickness, a rush of hallucinations overwhelmed me. The horrific images flashed violently in my mind's eye . . .

> *There was blood everywhere. It seeped through soil and flowed down the path like a brook of curdled gore. The smell of decay burned my nostrils and the landscape spun. I stood in a helpless daze until my legs gave out. I fell to my knees and a wave of black spiders overcame me. They crawled up my body and filled my mouth as I screamed with terror. A snake dropped down and twisted its silken body around my neck. My stomach convulsed and heaved. There was no air—no air in my lungs. I dragged and clawed my nails down my constricted neck. It was not working. The snake was too strong. It was stealing my life with no remorse. The serpent tightened its grip, and the darkness closed in.*

"Emilie . . ." Someone called my name. It was a faint cry from a distant place. "Emilie . . ." I knew that voice.

It was the ghost!

With a great deal of trouble, I stood up and stumbled forward. The lantern swung perilously in my hand as I staggered on uneasy feet. I felt intoxicated, poisoned, and close to death.

I heard my name again, "Emilie . . ." The ghost was too far away. He would never find me in time. The forest had changed, and I was waist deep in thick fog. It was too hard to see. Even my lantern fought and failed to penetrate the pitch-black.

With my last bit of strength, I managed to choke out a strangled plea. "Help me . . . help." I fell on my knees again, and the fog plumed out around me. It returned instantly to envelop my body and blind my senses.

I reached out for salvation as my body surrendered consciousness. Just before the darkness prevailed, a ghostly hand pushed through the mist. Like fate, our fingers interlaced. The electric shock that coursed through me revived my wilted spirit. The unearthly connection lifted me from the ground and pulled me through the fog. Next thing I knew, I was in the arms of the ghost. I looked up at my savior's face. His striking eyes blazed bright as he freed me from the dark. In my dazed state, the young man looked like a fearsome archangel. He was a celestial soldier sent to rescue me.

We managed to distance ourselves from the cabin and from the nightmares that shielded it. Miraculously, the lantern was still in my hand. Its glowing flame wrapped us in light as we walked in silence. The map was lost, but it did not matter. It did not matter, because I had *him*.

"You came for me." I finally was able to say in a fragile voice.

"You were in trouble! They must have seen you coming. Somehow, they can see," he said cryptically while pulling me along.

"Who are *they*?" I asked, but he did not answer. I looked up at the young man and saw him staring down at me. There was a spark of pain in his fiery eyes.

"Are you all right?" he asked.

Tears swelled in my eyes. I pressed my lips together to suppress the rising emotion. The spell that possessed me had lifted, but the hideous experience would scar me for life. The gruesome illusions would creep into my dreams and torment me for years to come. How could words express the chilling power that infected me?

The young man saw my face and knew the answer. He held me tight and whispered, "I'm sorry."

To change the subject, I took a few calming breaths and asked, "How did you appear this time?"

"The moon." He pointed to the sky. "I can feel the energy pour down to me." He looked down at his own body, as if he could hardly believe it himself. His image was so clear that he almost looked alive. Nevertheless, his touch was still electric and unlike any touch from the living.

The fog began to thin and wisp at our ankles. We approached the bridge and stopped on its crest. The river flowed steadily beneath our feet.

"Thank you," I said. "If not for you, who knows what would have happened. I was so scared. I thought I was going to die . . ."

He came close and hushed me with a fingertip. It tingled on my lips. He lingered there for a moment. The energy that drew us together was mesmerising. My heart pounded and my cheeks flushed. The ghost ran his finger gently down my chin. He traced it along the curve of my neck and collarbone, leaving a sweet tingle in its wake. With eyes cast down, his chest heaved. My own breath hitched as the phantom's breath cooled my heated skin. When I shivered, he took me in his arms. My head pitched back in response to the shock that charged through me. The current that flowed between us was so powerful. As is coursed through my veins, I could feel myself falling. I was falling under another spell—a spell of a different kind. It was natural and pure, but just as frightening.

The ghost looked at me through hooded eyes and whispered, "Let's go home, Emilie." His voice was a mix of yearning and heart-ache. He released me from the embrace and held my hand as we left the path. I had never been so happy to see a cemetery in all my life.

MOONLIT TRYST

The ghost guided me through the cemetery and onto the grounds of Kingsgrove. I stepped onto the grass and peered up at the full moon. It loomed brilliantly in the starry sky, allowing the young man to flourish in its light. His image did not waver and fade before me. Although he was still just a spirit, I could finally see him entirely.

The ghost was tall, with a lean build and broad shoulders. He wore a fitted vest over a button-down shirt, with the collar open and the sleeves rolled. His trousers sat high on his hips, and he wore shoes made of leather. His dark hair was thick and tousled, with the sides cut short. I imagined running my hands through it, and my heart skipped a beat. I could not take my eyes off of him. The smooth angles of his face were stunning. The young man was refined and handsome, but his clothes were twisted and torn. His hair was damp, and his skin was either dirty, or bruised, or both. It saddened me to see the ghost as he was at the moment of his death. It proved that his end was not such a peaceful one.

The ghost watched me in silence as I explored him with my eyes. I circled him quietly, and the lantern's flame leapt with the beat of my heart. I wanted to remember every detail. The spirit of a dead man was standing in front of me! It was more than a tender moment shared between us—it was a miracle.

Eventually, I bent over to place the lantern on the ground. A soft breeze blew my hair over my face, and I went to brush it away. The ghost knelt in the grass and stopped me. With a gentle hand, he swept the fair strands aside. In an instant, we were face to face. The sadness in his eyes made my chest tighten. He needed me, but I was afraid.

If I freed the ghost, would he move on to another place? Did that mean I would lose him forever—lose him just like everyone else before? It was selfish of me to want him to stay. He was suffering. Besides, I could not forget that he was dead. *He* was dead and *I* was alive.

I could not bear to see his sorrow any longer. It was a beautiful summer evening, and the moon had offered him a gift. I could have taken the opportunity to demand answers, but he avoided all my questions. Why? I searched his face as if it held the truth, but all I saw was pain. It would have been a shame to waste the moment on sadness. It was time to just let go.

We *had* to seize the night.

I took his face in my hands. My palms tingled, and our gaze met. I could see the spark of magic in his eyes and when his lips parted, my heart skipped once again. "You rescued me tonight from something so horrible. It's my turn to do something for you." My voice was just a whisper. "When was the last time you had a little fun?"

The ghost furrowed his brow. "I can't remember," he said with certainty. "You are the first person to come here and see me. It has been so long since I've been happy. It's hard to find joy when you're trapped in this place."

I looked right into his eyes and said, "Well . . . if you want to keep me here, you are going to have to catch me."

Before he could respond, I sprung from the ground and ran off into the darkness. A game of cat-and-mouse was on. Once the ghost realized what was happening, he was quick to chase after. The excitement was hard to hide as I giggled and weaved through the vast gardens. His unearthly laughter was close behind. The sound echoed through the air as it travelled between his world and mine.

My playful escape led me to the graveyard, where I crouched behind the willow tree. I was completely out of breath. All I could hear were my own gasps and airy giggles. I looked over my shoulder, around the trunk of the tree. My neck strained and my eyes squinted to see the yard past the cemetery gate. The ghost was nowhere in sight. As my breathing slowed, an empty silence closed in. The laughter that had lilted through the air moments before had vanished. All was still and quiet.

It was too quiet.

If the ghost had a name, I would have called out to him. I did not want to lose him again, as I had at Willowmere Lake. The moment he vanished, I felt more alone than ever before. That same sinking feeling grew inside of me as each second passed. I rested against the tree, and could feel the rough bark on my back. The stone angels stood gracefully before me. Their black shadows spilled onto the ground, like two distorted silhouettes. I could see their sombre gaze in the moonlight. They seemed to peer into my soul and ask, *What are you doing, Emilie?*

What was I doing?

Deep down, I knew that these feelings were dangerous. It was even more dangerous than sitting alone in the dark while the dead lay beneath me.

The realization of where I was began to fill me with dread. Six graves encircled me. Six bodies rested and rotted in pine, a mere six feet below the earth. I was still recovering from the spell that poisoned me by the Eventide's cabin. All the bravado I felt before was left behind in the woods. Panic trickled through my veins, just as something touched the top of my head. My imagination ran wild, and the phantom spiders had returned. Their long, greasy legs scurried through my hair as they crawled between the tangled strands. I cried out, frantically swatting at the empty space above me.

To my relief, there were no spiders. There was only a ghost sitting on low hanging branch. He laughed at my reaction while jumping silently to the ground. He crouched down so that we were face to face once again. We stayed that way for a moment. My heart raced from his sudden closeness. He looked at me with a straight face and said, "You're it," then ran off.

It took a moment to compose myself and rise to my feet. I was on a rollercoaster ride of chilling thrills and delight. He was still there . . . and I had to catch him. I did not want to lose him ever again.

I spotted the lantern over in the grass, ran for it, and grasped the metal handle. I raised the wick to brighten the flame and held it up. The young man was already hidden in the shadows.

Just as the chase began, I heard music. The distant song was haunting and beautiful. Adalynn was playing one of her old records. The melody poured out of the parlor window and drifted clear across the property.

The playful laughter had faded and the energy in the air thickened. The pursuit had a new intensity. As I wandered through the yard, fireflies sparked and flickered around me. Their tiny lights guided my way and beckoned me to the garden. I entered through a leafy trellis and my body was enveloped by flowers and ornamental foliage. I weaved my way through the maze of plants. Petals and leaves caressed my bare skin, heightening my senses.

Music hummed in my ears while the full moon shone brilliantly in the sky. The atmosphere was extraordinary. All that was missing . . . was the ghost. I was sure that he knew *exactly* where I was. The garden provided many shadows and corners for hiding. The young man would be found only when *he* was ready to reveal himself. I was clearly at a disadvantage. There was nothing magical about me. The ghost was entwined and trapped between space and time, forever handsome and young. He harnessed the energy around him and consumed me with his power. I was just an average and ordinary girl. There was only one thing that I had, that he did not—I had life.

Suddenly, I shivered and my eyes watered. There was a familiar energy radiating behind me. Even though I anticipated him before turning, I still jumped. The lantern fell from my hand and landed upright in the grass.

The ghost captured me in his arms and sent a shock of electricity to every nerve in my body. The jolt made my knees weak as he lowered me gently to the ground. "Emilie," he breathed my name, voice heavy with desire. "Remarkable girl. You have come here to save me from this hell." He grabbed a fistful of his shirt, right above his chest and over his heart. "I already feel you here."

I lay there on the grass, helpless beneath him. He held himself over me and his hazel eyes blazed bright. They were full of passion—they were full of life. How did I ever believe he was without life? There he was, overflowing with more of it than I ever had. *I* was the one who had been dead the entire time. *I* was not even awake before then, let alone alive.

Even if the ghost was no longer living in this world, he was living somewhere just beyond it. I had to find out where that was to help him move on. Even if it meant losing him, I had to make that sacrifice. As much as it tore my heart in pieces, there was no other way. He had been trapped for too many years. If I freed him, I would be trapped in a world without him for many years to follow. That was life, unfortunately. No matter how hard you fought for those who mattered, they always left in the end.

I could not change the scary things to come. In the spirit of seizing the night, I chose to ignore the inevitable. There was only me and him, and that precious moment. *That* was what mattered most.

A single tear fell from the corner of my eye. A tear that had been locked away, for fear of all the pain it held. It was a terrible mistake, yet there was no stopping it from falling. For some reason, I wanted to let it go—I wanted to let him in.

Resting a hand above my heart, I whispered, "I feel you too . . ."

The ghost took the back of his hand and grazed it over my freckled cheek. His eyes were eager as they travelled to my mouth. My lips parted in response. A white-hot energy burned between us. He lowered his face to mine, and my heart pounded with fear and anticipation. When our lips met, the sensation was overwhelming. My back arched with every electrical charge that pulsed through me. The ghost wrapped me inside of his strong arms. I was his prisoner.

As his cool lips moved with mine, tasting of mint and tonic, I knew that no other kiss could compare. The sensation was strange, dizzying and all consuming. My thoughts and emotions tumbled and spiralled. The experience could not be formed and focused into words or rational thoughts; it all happened too quickly. There was no way to prepare for such an extraordinary thing. I was not kissing a living man. I was kissing a dead man whose spirit was alive.

The ghost took possession of my body. He left me shattered and breathless. I took his face in my hands and reluctantly drew back. At that moment, the energy between us shifted. The electricity was gone. His face was suddenly smooth and hard to the touch. It felt strange and different. I opened my eyes to see what changed, and was horrified by what I discovered. The ghost was gone, and in my hands was a human skull. Two empty sockets gaped down at me, and the jawbone was slack. I screamed, and the skull began to crumble and turn to ash. I turned away to avoid the falling remnants. It burned my eyes and choked the back of my throat. The grit tasted so foul that I gagged and sat up coughing. With the sleeve of my shirt, I rubbed away the vile remains. Once my sight returned, I looked down at my hands. The ash was gone. The taste in my mouth was gone.

It was all gone! All, except for the lingering burn on my lips.

The ghost had left me again. Something or someone was trying to push him away. Was it the same force holding him captive—entrapping him between this world and the next? Did the same force prevent me from finding the Eventide's cabin?

What exactly was I up against?

Clearly, I did not understand the deep-rooted magic that lived in Willow Vale. I was faced with the unknown, the indefinite, and the uncertain. The unknown was always a bit frightening, but that was not what worried me most. What worried me most was how the *ghost* had bewitched me. I could not fight it any longer, and *that* was truly terrifying.

SOAKED IN CRIMSON

I was up to my neck in hot water. It was early Monday morning, before the sunrise and before the moonset. My skin was scrubbed raw with soap and my body lied paralyzed in the clawfoot tub. I did not dare to close my eyes. It was the only way to escape my thoughts and all the morbid creatures lurking there. Sleep was not an option. Nightmares were waiting for me, and I refused to enter them willingly.

For the entire night, I waited foolishly for the ghost to return. I even opened the curtains to let the moonlight in, ran water, and turned on every light. It was not enough. I felt and saw nothing.

I was not in the mood to spend time with Adalynn that day. I still felt the lingering effects of the previous night. Even as I lay in hot water, wave after wave of icy chills passed through my shaken body. My blood still flowed with conjured toxins. I just wanted to stay hidden away until the sickness passed. My sanity depended on it.

It was only my second week living in Willow Vale, and I could hardly believe it. So much had happened in such a short time. My old life was forgotten. My grandmother's memory would always be in my heart, but everything else had completely disappeared. It was all irrelevant, unimportant, and insignificant next to the new world I had discovered.

My life had become more dangerous than I ever dreamt possible. I was living in a haunted house, engrossed in an old mystery that was possibly tangled up in some strange local magic. These things were found between the pages of a book! I did not possess the knowledge or power to fight something so unimaginable. An unseen force attacked me in the woods and removed all my self-control. It was more than a simple parlor trick—it was a dark, cruel warning that would not be soon forgotten.

The ghost was right. There was something or someone who was desperate to keep him trapped. He rescued me from the violent delusions in the woods. He swept me up and delivered me from a life void of excitement and passion. All that I could offer him in return was my devotion. I was devoted to fight, and win. I knew I would lose him in the process, but it was not about me. It was about a young man's eternal freedom.

There was a reason why I found JoJo's want-ad and became the caretaker of Kingsgrove. There was a reason why I did not pass by that bulletin board, just like every other day. The ghost had said I was the first person he could see, and the first that could see him in return. That meant something! Our fates had crossed, and I refused to fail him—not for anything in the world.

✗ ✗ ✗

Bitter steam enveloped my face as I eagerly drank my morning coffee. The hot, black liquid did very little to lift the heavy feeling of exhaustion. I blinked, feeling the burn of tired eyes. My head was pounding. I put my mug down on the table and rubbed my aching temples. Thankfully, the kitchen was quiet, except for all the sprightly birds that sang through the open window. Their chipper tune annoyed me. I picked up my coffee, blew the steam away, and took another sip.

Adalynn sat across from me in silence while I stared at her. All the answers were locked away in her mind—I was certain of it. How could she just sit there and do nothing? I felt like shaking her. She almost drowned over fifty years ago! Why did she spend the rest of her life living in fear?

It was hard to believe that a privileged woman such as Miss King was not offered enough love and support to recover. Adalynn *chose* to exist in silence. She just gave up and wasted her second chance.

At that moment, I could not control my rising frustration. I was tired of hopelessly beating on a brick wall made of secrets. Adalynn knew that Kingsgrove was haunted. In one way or another, she knew the young man was there. The truth was in her eyes, yet she did not seem to care.

With a narrow gaze, I looked over the brim of my mug and said, "I see him, you know?" Adalynn looked up from her breakfast, and our eyes met. Hers were wide, but her expression was blank and revealed nothing. "Who is he Ada?" I put my mug down and rested my palms on the table. I leaned in close and waited. Her lips were sealed tight. She did not even blink. I tried again. "Why is he here?" My frustration was starting to show. Miss King continued to hold onto her stubborn silence. I lost my cool and smacked my hands down on the table. The dishes rattled and Adalynn's cup tipped over, spilling tea into its saucer. I stood up, knocking my chair to the floor, and got right in her face. "Tell me Ada! Please!" I sounded desperate, tired, and crazy all at once.

Adalynn jumped back in her seat, clearly frightened by my sudden outburst. She looked so timid and fragile that my heart flooded instantly with regret. Tears filled my eyes and I choked out, "I'm sorry Ada." I went around the table and kneeled beside her on the floor. The warm tears spilled down my cheeks. I looked up and held her hands in mine. "I don't know what I was thinking. I'm so sorry. I know you can't tell me the things I need to know. I feel like . . . like . . . I've lost my mind."

Miss King pulled her hands free, and I waited for her to push me away. To my surprise, she rested my head onto her lap instead. Despite my actions, the woman gently stroked my hair to soothe me. The gesture was full of affection and understanding. It made me feel like that little girl again—so young and vulnerable in a troubled world.

My crying was lulled and the exhaustion took hold. Adalynn stood me up and slowly led me to the great room. I curled up on the chaise lounge and hugged a satin pillow tight to my chest. The woman covered me with a thin blanket and closed the heavy curtains. The morning light was hidden, and room was coated in darkness. I heard the floorboards creak as Adalynn passed by. When the double doors closed behind her, my subconscious took over. I was thrown down a dark hole—down, down, down a sinking abyss. My body slept deeply and fitfully as my mind crashed right into another nightmare . . .

I was crouched in the rafters of an old cabin while looking down at the room below. The young man was there. Everything about him was the same, from his damp hair to his dirty clothes. He was right there, but I could not climb down or call out to him. I was only a silent observer, hiding in a memory.

It was my turn to be the ghost.

The young man sat, hunched over in a wooden chair. His head hung lifelessly and he bled from a small gash on the palm of his hand. It dripped slowly into a tiny pool of crimson by his left foot. I thought he was already dead, but then noticed the gentle rise and fall of shallow breathing.

A nearby hearth was lit. The flames sparked and crackled as they consumed what looked like a bundle of herbs. The dense smoke lingered with me high in the timbers.

A young teenage girl entered the cabin. She was tall and slender, wearing a simple navy blue dress and sweater. It was a poor fit and was draped awkwardly over her thin frame. Her long, black hair hung tangled over her pretty face, and her bare feet were stained with dirt. The girl stared at the young man—her eyes raged with hatred. She began to circle him, like a predator stalking its prey. With a disturbed smile on her face, she began to chant.

"Concede mortem ad cubiculum, obscuro infinitum. Pueri spiritus redeat ad corpus."

Over and over, she recited the chant, getting louder as she went on. Her voice sounded less human and more bestial as she repeated the eerie mantra.

Finally, she stopped and viscously grabbed a fistful of the young man's hair. The girl wrenched his head back and leaned in until she was face to face with her victim. He groaned and winced, but did not have the power to fight her.

Through clenched teeth, the girl spat out, "Goodbye, my love," and kissed him hard on the lips.

I woke abruptly and nearly fell from the chaise lounge. My vision was blurred and my eyes were swollen and dry. I rubbed them and blinked until the great room was revealed. Dust motes danced along a single streak of daylight. The hot summer light had escaped the drawn curtains and hit the floor at my feet. I did not move until I felt the pinch of heat. The sun burnt my skin, like the dream burned in my mind. The chant was seared to my memory. I would never forget those words and how they flowed from the girl's mouth like venom. The words *Mortem, Spiritus* and *Corpus* were easy enough to understand, but what they meant all strung together, was not so. The language sounded archaic, like Latin. Yes, Latin! I had to find someone who spoke the old language. That, or find someone who had the recourses to translate it. Ruby Monrose instantly came to mind. The Willow Vale librarian was my only hope.

While climbing the massive stairway to the east wing, I thought about all the nightmares. Was the ghost trying to untangle a twisted story in my unconscious mind? These were not just dreams. They were small fragments of clouded memories and dark moments from the past. The nightmares were interlaced with little hints of the truth—the truth about what happened. The girl in the cabin was either responsible or connected to his death. I saw the look in her eyes. I saw the way she hated him. She hated him, yet she called him *my love* and kissed him. The sour ache of jealousy invaded my heart as I recalled her vile embrace.

I found Mr. King's office and sat at his desk. I pivoted toward the window in the impressive, antique leather chair. The setting sun peeked through the trees as the grandfather clock struck seven. The chimes echoed through the halls to salute the coming night. I turned around, grabbed a fountain pen, and wrote down the Latin chant. The foreign words stared up at me, baffling me even more on paper. After a while, they seemed to blur together and lose their meaning entirely. I tore the note into many little pieces then threw it away. I watched the paper fall like snow to the bottom of the waste bin before leaving the room.

The Latin chant was significant. It had *something* to do with young man's death. I hated all those words, and wanted to understand them just as much. Unfortunately, it was only Monday night, meaning Saturday was a long way off. I had a job to do, and the library would have to wait. Besides, I had to find Adalynn to apologize again for my outburst. I was embarrassed and worried that my behavior would get me fired and sent away. My job was to help her, not question her silence. The thought of leaving was unbearable, and the anxiety put my stomach in knots.

Miss King was playing solitaire in the kitchen when I found her. I hesitated in the doorway and fussed with my locket. Adalynn just looked up at me and smiled. She rose from her chair and grabbed a plate of food that was warming in the oven. She brought it to the dining room and placed it next to two glasses of red wine. Adalynn made me supper! She waved me over to take a seat, and I exhaled slightly with relief.

I sat across from her and started to eat. The first bite hit my nervous stomach like a rock. The food was warm and rich with southern comfort, but I was still sick with regret. After staring down at my plate for some time, I finally found the courage to apologize. "I've been a horrible companion to you Ada. I'm *so sorry* about this morning."

Adalynn made a gesture with her hand, as if to say that everything was already forgotten. To lay it to rest, we raised our glasses. The rims tinged as we toasted to friendship. I welcomed the dark liquid as it washed away all the bitter feelings.

Yes, it was frustrating that Adalynn could not speak. She had her reasons to stay silent, and it was not my place to condemn her for it. It was hard to understand the eccentric woman that hid away in Willow Vale. She was a strange person and Kingsgrove was a strange place, but it was all I had . . . apart from the ghost.

Of course, I could not forget the ghost. We had a connection that transcended life and death, but in the end, it did not matter. The young man would always be out of reach, and if I managed to save him, it would all be over forever. I would never see him again, at least not until my own body rested six feet underground. Until that day came, I would have to look back and cherish what little time we had. The moment we shared the night before was extraordinary. Those few precious minutes were locked away in my heart like a jewel in a box of hidden secrets.

I took my last bite of dinner and swallowed all my misery. I buried it deep, and washed it down with wine. Miss King poured us a second glass and I followed her gaze out the window. As the night air flowed through the open pane, an idea came to mind. "Let's do something special tomorrow. Why don't we go for a walk? You could choose a place nearby. We could have a picnic." Ada took a moment to consider and eventually nodded in agreement.

For the rest of the evening, I read from *The Old Farmer's Almanac* and played cards with Miss King. Once the grandfather clock chimed out the eleventh hour, she left me alone for the night. As I tidied up, the creaks and cries of Kingsgrove were my only companions. The house shifted and cracked its old wooden bones throughout the night, every night. I hummed a quiet melody to mask the sounds and hide my rising discomfort.

Before long, I was climbing the stairs to my room. I stepped up to the first landing and stood centered between the east and west wing. The large gilded mirror loomed over me. The surface waved like a calm pool of molten silver. I took a few steps closer, and the mirror displayed my reflection with brutal honesty.

My blue eyes were wilted with exhaustion. I ran my hands over my freckled face, leaned in, and puckered my lips. They were stained red from the wine. I rubbed them with the sleeve of my shirt, and then, in an instant, my body flash froze with fear. All the blood drained from my face, like a spilled glass of merlot. A face appeared over my shoulder in the mirror. I shrieked and spun to see a lucid phantom standing behind me. It was not the young man; it was the teenage girl from my dream! She was a few years older, but I knew that face and those evil eyes anywhere.

The young woman had long, black hair that hung around her like a grisly cape. She wore a white nightgown soaked in blood. It dripped gruesomely from the hem and spattered on the floor. The horror was magnified with every *tap . . . tap . . . tap.*

I stood petrified and vulnerable with my fear fully exposed. She stared at me with a face twisted in pure hatred. Her dark eyes were ablaze with bitter hostility. She looked like a broken doll, as she twitched and flickered before me. Without warning, she rushed forward and we collided brutally. Her energy hit me like a frigid block of ice. The wind was knocked out of me, and I collapsed on the floor. I curled into the fetal position until I was able to draw the first painful breath. Somehow, I managed to sit up, scurry away, and press my back against the wall beneath the mirror. While gasping hysterically, my eyes darted around the poorly lit stairway.

The woman's ghost had vanished.

Eventually, the ache in my stomach faded away, and I staggered up to my room. Anyone else would have bolted for the front door. I chose to stay. No matter what Kingsgrove threw at me, I would never run from it again.

If the woman was trying to scare me, she had succeeded. I felt ravaged by the sudden attack. My weak knees hindered the frantic escape to my room. While looking behind me, I tripped and stumbled on the stairs.

As I rushed through the hallways of the west wing, a door creaked open. It stopped me dead in my tracks. The light in the storage room was on, and it spilled into the dark corridor. After fearfully glancing over both shoulders, I dared to look in. The room felt surprisingly safe. The energy that I had come to know well mingled with the dusty air. It belonged to the young man. Although it was cool and electric like the woman's spirit, his presence was not nearly as dark and glacial.

I entered and my heart raced. The atmosphere was ignited. All my senses were jarred to life by his presence—except for my sense of sight. I could feel him all around me, but I could not see him with my eyes.

DROWNED MAGNOLIA

"**G**host?" My voice was softened by the lofty stacks of cardboard. "Where are you?" There was no reply. The air hummed with electricity, and time ticked on . . . *tick, tick, tick* . . . but nothing changed.

The ghost did not appear, yet he lured me there for some reason.

My eyes explored the many dusty boxes then came across a large wooden chest. I opened that same chest a week before and found nothing but old linens. A pleasant chill washed over me and enticed me to look again. I sat cross-legged on the floor and unlatched the trunk a second time. I raised the lid and the hinges cried out. Feathery dust plumed and spiralled before my eyes. My nose twitched as the smell of must and old mothballs irked my senses.

As I suspected, the same linens were stacked and folded on the surface, but this time I dug a little deeper, and sure enough, there was more! Lying beneath the delicate fabrics was a stash of antique scrapbooks and photo albums. Ever so gently, I lifted them out and laid them on the floor.

An elegant wedding album stood out amongst the rest. I took it in my lap. It was filled with beautiful, sepia-toned photographs, each airbrushed to perfection. Jonathan and Evelyn King looked sophisticated in their lavish clothing from the early 1900s. It was sad to think that these young, beautiful people were now merely dust and bone.

One by one, I flipped through the vintage mementos. The room seemed to fade away as I blissfully fell back to a long-forgotten time. My mind was captivated by the King's opulent past. Their lives were truly rich in more ways than one.

Eventually, I put the family albums aside when a particular baby book caught my eye. I ran my hand over the cover and felt the tiny rosebud embellishments under my fingertips. It was such a sweet and delicate little book. The spine was held together with silk ribbon and tide with a flattened bow. The inside was inscribed, *Adalynn King, Born April 22nd, 1935.*

Every snapshot and caption was a glimpse into the first year of Miss King's life. Her older siblings were with her in nearly every photograph. The girls cradled baby Ada ever so proudly in their arms. They obviously cherished their little sister, unconditionally. How could they not? She was a precious baby girl, decorated in lace with a curl of hair atop her head. Her angelic eyes looked up at me with pure wonderment. Little Adalynn awaited a world that she would never venture into. The innocence was bittersweet.

With Miss King's book in hand, I could feel the rhythmic pulse of the ghost's energy surround me. While teetering between two worlds, he coaxed me to look a little deeper, but all I noticed were a few photographs missing from the pages. A faint shadow of where they once were still marked the paper. Had they fallen out? I leaned over and rummaged through the trunk again. There was nothing, so I shrugged it off and glanced through the other baby books. They were all pleasantly worn and faded with newborn girls, wrapped in fine lace and swaddled in loving arms.

While gathering up the albums, I found another scrapbook that was overlooked before. It was quite old and more fragile than all the rest. The cover was trimmed with golden ivy and a lone white bird flew in the center. I carefully opened it to find the book was empty. All that remained, pressed between the pages, was a dried-up magnolia. The keepsake slid from the book and crumbled in my lap. I tried to salvage the flower, but only managed to destroy it instead. I sadly placed the little pieces between the pages and sealed it back inside.

As I went to put the empty scrapbook away, a cool breeze whirled around me and sent my loose hair in turmoil. In an instant, the hum of energy vanished and the ghost was gone. I looked down at the book that rested in my hands. The young man guided me there and all I found were blank pages—all I found were more obscure, empty clues to solve a twisted riddle.

✗ ✗ ✗

That evening I slept with the lights on and hid beneath the covers like an absolute coward. After meeting the ghost of the young man, I believed that he haunted Kingsgrove alone. I was wrong. There was a woman with him, and she was angry. She did not search for freedom—she searched for blood.

Had I provoked her by helping the young man? In the dream, she loathed and tortured him without remorse. She played a role in his death, and there I was, searching for the truth. I was a threat.

I shivered under the covers and glanced at the old, empty scrapbook on my desk. I had decided to keep it close, because it got me thinking. There was something significant hidden inside, without a doubt. The flimsy pages were yellowed with square shaped patches throughout. It seemed that the original photographs were ripped out and stolen long-ago. In fact, the entire house looked the same way! I noticed all the empty frames hanging on walls and sitting on shelves. Now the family albums were missing their pictures as well. I wondered if it was all connected. Someone was hiding something, and it did not surprise me in the least. Kingsgrove may have once been a structure built with wood and stone, but the *creature* it had become was built with secrets and suffering.

I tossed and turned, falling in and out of consciousness until daybreak. The morning sun scared off the night and drew me out of my quilted refuge. I dressed quickly and found Miss King on her way to the kitchen. My plan was to spend the whole day with her, partially out of guilt, and partially out of fear. I did not want to be alone. The possibility of another encounter with the grisly phantom terrified me.

Thankfully, the day granted us crystal-blue skies and warm fragrant breezes. We lingered happily in the garden until our stomachs growled. I ventured inside to find a picnic basket while Adalynn went upstairs to freshen up. Before long, our lunch was packed along with a graphite pencil and sketchbook. I needed to find some inspiration—a muse—a distraction. The bloody woman and her evil eyes were still vivid in my mind, but I would not draw her. Drawing the phantom would make her far too real. I refused to acknowledge her that way. I refused to give her that power.

I brought the picnic basket to the foyer and crouched to tie my sneakers. Out of habit, I touched my necklace and felt my pockets for the rusty knife. As my hand rested over the ivory handle, the staircase creaked. My head shot up.

Was it the phantom?

No, it was Adalynn. She was on the landing, adjusting her straw hat in the mirror. My heart pounded as my nerves hung dangerously on edge. I stood up and breathed deep to hide the panic that trembled through my body.

Miss King turned and smiled when she saw me waiting by the door. Together, we left the house and walked the stone drive to Kings Lane. I followed her along the dirt road with the basket swinging at my side. After a short distance, Adalynn took me down an old trail that led into the woods. The balmy air soothed my soul as we hiked along the hidden path.

Willow Vale was very different from my hometown. I came from a cookie-cutter suburb on the edge of a paved, neon metropolis. It was easy to get caught up in the fast-paced lifestyle, but the city was cold and hard. Willow Vale was warm and soft; it gave me a reason to slow down. I could never go back. Even though my new life was a dangerous cocktail of mystery and mayhem, it had hints of intrigue and passion. I would not leave, no matter what happened in the end.

Where the path ended, marshland began. An everglade spanned the landscape, taking my breath away. Glassy, dark water soaked the forest floor and seeped between the ferns that brushed against our ankles. Seeing the marsh from Kings Lane through the window of my Trans Am was nothing in comparison. The backwoods of Willow Vale belonged inside a gothic novel on some musty wooden bookshelf somewhere. It was bewitching. Sketchbook hugged tight to my chest, I breathed in the earthy air. The atmosphere lured me in like a hypnotised snake following a charmer's flute.

My skin tingled with curiosity as Adalynn left the path and pulled me through the soggy ferns. Where was she taking me? I followed her close and watched her feet move knowingly along the water's edge. Before long, we came to a small clearing, hemmed with willows and draped in Spanish moss. An old rowboat was overturned next to the leafy aperture. With a coy smile, the woman gestured over to it.

"You want to go out in that?" I asked surprised. A boat ride was not at all what I had expected.

She nodded *yes* in response, so I proceeded to turn the boat rightside up. As I brushed off the cobwebs, a familiar engraving appeared at the stern. Eight spears in a starburst pattern were crudely etched into the wood. Ruby Monrose wore the same emblem, in silver, at her neck. How strange, I thought in passing, then swiped at a beetle that scurried up my arm.

After stowing the basket in the bottom of the boat, I managed to shove it halfway down the bank. The bow bobbed in the water as the stern gripped the bank. I attached the oars and held the shell steady so Adalynn could climb in. She took a seat, and then I pushed with all my strength. Before the boat floated off, I hopped in and steadied it in the water.

"Ok, here we go," I said nervously, taking the oars in hand. The rowing motion felt strange at first, and it took some time to get the hang of it. Adalynn did not seem to notice my awkward strokes. She sat contently with her back against the seat, eating a cucumber sandwich.

Eventually, we floated amongst a sunken grove of bald cypress trees. Their splayed roots clung to the calm, dark surface. The setting was eerie, yet peaceful, so I lifted the oars from the water and let the boat glide freely. We quietly ate our picnic while drifting in the heart of the everglade.

It surprised me how relaxed Adalynn was on the open water. The woman had been an eccentric recluse ever since she nearly drowned in a river. It traumatised her so badly that she never spoke again. She locked herself away in Kingsgrove and never learned to read or write. She never married, nor had any children—all because her life was threatened by *water*. Yet there she was, completely at ease in that tired, old boat. So much so, that she curled up with her blanket and actually fell asleep.

Before she woke, I picked up my sketchbook and began to draw her sleeping portrait. With a swift hand, I mimicked the lines and curls of her delicate features in lead. My pencil traced her wisps of loose hair, which spilled over her shoulders in gentle silver waves. Adalynn's beauty was refined and ageless, especially with her face softened with sleep. I did all I could to capture the peaceful moment on paper.

As I drew the oval line for the brim of her hat, the boat knocked against something in the water. It rocked from the hit, causing my pencil to slip. I sighed with frustration and scowled at the messy line. Adalynn shifted in her seat, but did not rouse. I craned my neck to see over the edge, and squinted through the waters reflecting light. In an instant, my heart stopped and dropped to the pit of my stomach. The face of a child appeared below the surface! Her thick hair flowed over her, like a graceful crown of bronze fire. The girl's dull, hazel eyes were wide with fear. She was stiff and pale, like a discarded doll sinking in a watery grave.

"Oh my God!" I was horrified.

The drawing fell from my hand and landed in the bottom of the boat. I plunged my arms into the water to rescue the little girl. She was so close. The boat tilted severely as I reached over the edge. With desperation, I clawed beneath the surface. My hands passed right through the girl. She disappeared! Her body dissolved and faded into the murky water, but I refused to give up on her. What if the downing girl had not simply vanished—what if she was sinking further down?

"No! No! No!" I repeated hysterically while attempting to stand in the rocking boat.

My racing heart told me to jump. My heart was telling me to save the little girl.

Before I dove into the everglade, someone grabbed hold of my leg. It was Adalynn. "Ada! There's a little girl in the water! She's drowning! I need to help her before it's too late!" I pulled against the woman's hold and tried to jump again. She clutched desperately onto my clothes in attempt to stop me. I looked back at her in panic. "Ada! Don't stop me . . . the girl!"

Miss King fiercely shook her head *no,* and gestured sternly for me to sit back down.

"But the girl . . ." I cried, wanting her to let go, and wanting her to understand my need to save the girl—to save someone.

Again, Miss King shook her head *no,* and held tight to my clothing.

We stared each other down until it slowly dawned on me. The realization felt like ice trailing bitterly down my spine. "There is no girl . . . is there?"

A simple shake of the woman's head was my answer. I sat heavily in my seat and pressed my eyes shut in exasperation. I rested my head in my hands and breathed heavily to slow my rushing adrenaline.

The girl looked so real and so young. Her empty, hazel stare pierced through my mind and sickened my stomach. She was *another* ghost, and *another* twisted layer in this messed up world of Kings.

I opened my eyes and narrowed them against the radiant sun. Another pair of hazel eyes stared back anxiously; unlike the little girl's dull gaze, they were alive and brimmed with compassion. Adalynn handed me an open bottle of sparkling water. I took it from her and gladly swallowed great mouthfuls to quench my depleting spirit. The water fizzed painfully in my throat, offering a brief distraction from the new terrors that haunted me.

BROKEN MADNESS

That evening, Miss King and I stayed in the east parlor. She sat quietly on the window seat as I read Williams Shakespeare's *Twelfth Night*. I found myself lost in the whimsical romance. The lines flowed poetically from my lips.

"A spirit I am indeed;
But am in that dimension grossly clad
Which from the womb I did participate.
Were you a woman, as the rest goes even,
I should my tears let fall upon your cheek,
And say 'Thrice-welcome, drowned Viola!'"

Viola believed her brother Sebastian was lost at sea, where a ship captain then rescued her. Viola cunningly disguised herself to serve the Duke Orsino. As the play went on, Viola fell in love with the Duke, and a tangled tale of misplaced affection began to unravel. By the end, Sebastian returned alive and married a wealthy countess. Viola then revealed her true self, and the Duke discovered his latent love for her.

The play was full of charming twists and turns with a pleasant outcome. It seemed contrary to my own story. I longed for my ending to be a happy one, like the *Twelfth Night*. I hoped it would not end in tragedy, like the many other works of Shakespeare.

My ghost had not returned since our kiss in the garden. I wondered why he was so close, yet so far away at the same time. The cool tingle of his presence had flushed my skin every now and again. He even manipulated the energy in the air to coax and guide me along, as promised. But I longed to see him—to touch him with my hands, and to lose myself in his phantom arms.

A war between logic and irrationality raged on inside of me. I had hopelessly fallen for a dead man, but I was no fool. We were not meant to be together. He was from a different time—a completely different world! Even if, by some impossible miracle, we had a chance, he may not feel the same affection in return.

Doubt crept into my body like a disease as each minute ticked by. My chest tightened into a knot that would not give. Feeling so out of control was both extraordinary and painful. I tried to swallow the pain as I read out loud, and practically choked on the words.

"He named Sebastian: I my brother know
Yet living in my glass; even such and so
In favor was my brother, and he went
Still in this fashion, color, ornament,
For him I imitate: O, if it prove,
Tempests are kind and salt waves fresh in love."

Adalynn smiled peacefully with her eyes closed as she savored every word. Only a few pages remained, but the ache in my chest was exhausting and Shakespeare's poetry started to blur. Walking over to the bookshelf, I marked the page with a silk ribbon, and slid *Twelfth Night* back between *Romeo and Juliet*, and *A Midsummer's Night Dream*.

Miss King woke from her daze and rose from her seat. Stiffly, she crossed the room to turn off the light. We left the darkened parlor together and walked up the grand staircase to the landing. We had hardly spent a moment apart for the entire day. Dread stirred inside of me as the time came to leave her side.

"Goodnight Ada." The anxiety was barely hidden from my voice. Miss King gave my arm a gentle squeeze before she disappeared into the east wing.

As I climbed the creaky steps to my room, my imagination ran wild. In an instant, the walls began to warp and close in around me. My nerves shattered into a trillion pieces and my skin crawled with fright. I felt the shadows stalk me, tease me, and taunt me, with their smoky fingers feeling my neck and stroking my hair. Walking swiftly, I tried to escape them, but my legs went weak. I stumbled and careened through the dark as the shadows whispered. Their icy breath caressed my face and chilled me to the bone.

Finally, my room appeared at the end of the corridor. I flung myself inside and slammed the door behind me. My heart raced and fluttered like a trapped bird beating its frantic wings inside my ribcage. The phantom woman and the drowning girl had me thoroughly unhinged. How could I continue to fight while fear wreaked havoc on my mind and body? My trembling hand rested over the locket at my neck, but the silver hawk only reminded me of all the strength I *did not* have.

"Where are you?" My plea hung glaringly in the empty room. It sounded so pathetic.

Could the ghost hear me? Could he hear the desperation?

I hated the weakness that burrowed a deep hole inside of me. My last bit of strength was quickly fading. I watched the hours pass and the minutes tick by while falling further and further away from the truth. The ghost sent me clues at every turn, but I failed to piece them all together.

A wall of doubt grew infinitely high with every tinge of fear that plagued me. Was it possible that the ghost had made a mistake? He obviously chose the wrong person to free him. It had to be true. He chose the wrong girl!

Panic slithered through my veins, and I could no longer breathe. I was suffocating on my own insecurities. I sprinted across the room and wrenched open the window. With a tight hold on the sill, I hung my head outside and filled my constricted lungs. The starry sky winked overhead as the night air sedated me.

Once the panic loosened its grip, I lay back on the bed and sank into the puffy quilt. After a long exhale, I went to rub my aching temples, but stopped with both hands just above my face. To my surprise, my palms were dusted in fine white crystals.

Where did it come from?

Then I remembered leaning out the window and stood up to look at the sill. Sure enough, the same white grit was spread along the bottom of the wooden frame. I pinched some between my fingers and sprinkled it into my palm. The granules gathered in the middle. I sniffed it then reluctantly touched it to the tip of my tongue.

Just what I thought—salt!

I remembered seeing packets of Drive-away Salt at *The Eventide Emporium*, so the real question was, *Who was in my room*? Only two women came to mind. I suspected JoJo Peters or Adalynn King was responsible. But why would either one do such a thing? Was the salt placed there to ward off evil? Was it a gesture meant to protect me?

What did it mean?

It meant someone practiced these strange rituals and believed in the local superstations. It meant someone believed that *I* needed protecting! There was only one woman that knew about the haunting of Kingsgrove. It seemed that Adalynn was hiding more than a few secrets, after all.

✗ ✗ ✗

The scribbling of lead on sketch-paper soothed me late into the night. As I fine-tuned the details of Adalynn's sleeping portrait, my fears were forgotten. For a fleeting moment, my mind was at peace. As a result, I eventually fell into a deep and dreamless sleep. When

I woke at dawn, my body was still propped with pillows. Even the sketchbook was still laid open in my lap.

Outside, the overcast sky was a dismal shade of grey. My mood was just as dark. Still, I forced myself out of bed. After all, the new day came with a new purpose. The old house was due for a cleaning. Every dusty nook and cranny and every shadowed corner was mine to explore. Finding Drive-Away Salt in the window was just the beginning. There was more to Kingsgrove and its mistress than it may have seemed.

After a quick bath, I slipped into some jeans, a blouse, and a pair of old moccasins. I brushed the tangles from my hair and watched the wet strands cascade down my back. In the mirror, my reflection was tragic. My face revealed the truth—this living-nightmare was ruining me. It was stealing my light. Darkness was closing in like storm clouds writhing in the sky. Fortunately, the willpower to go on still lingered . . . somewhere. With blue eyes narrowed, I summoned what strength I had left, but it was all in vain. Despite my best efforts, anxiety mounted as I left the false security of my bedroom. With fists clenched at my sides, I bit my bottom lip and entered the dreary hallway. My heart thumped every time my feet made contact with the hardwood floor. I stared straight ahead and focused on each hollow *thump . . . thump . . . thump,* until my eyes rested on Adalynn. She was already in the kitchen preparing a small meal for two.

We ate in the dining room and listened to the soft hush of rain on the rooftop. The *Willow Vale Gazette* predicted bad weather from morning until night. It made no difference one way or the other. Staying inside to snoop around Kingsgrove was all I had in mind, even if the thought of wandering around alone still terrified me. Who knew what I would find. Or who would find me, for that matter.

As I washed the dishes, Miss King took her basket of yarn out to the veranda. Standing on my tippy-toes, I peeked through the open window. The woman was rocking in the porch swing while knitting a jade-green afghan. This was my chance to find what she was hiding.

With cleaning supplies in hand, I started to shine and dust the old estate. As expected, every windowsill and outside door was freshly lined with salt. Miss King was feeling vulnerable, without a doubt, for not a single threshold was left unprotected.

Moments later, while sweeping the entryway closet, something else caught my eye. Nestled in the corner, lying next to a half-melted candle was a locket of hair. The strands were light blonde, and tied with a wisp of thread. Straight away, I knew the hair was mine. I choked back the gasp that lurched in my throat. My eyes stared wide and unblinking at the simple yet unsettling display.

Was it a spell—a spell attached to me?

Without disturbing a single thing, I slowly backed away and shut the closet door. I already learned my lesson with these sorts of charms in the woods. That night, my curiously ended with a hideous spell cast over me. Without the knowledge, I would not meddle with any of it ever again.

Finding the salt and locket of hair fueled my search. With determination, I walked the narrow hallway behind the staircase and stopped at the basement door. My thoughts fell back to that fateful night when the ghost first manifested. That night, he terrified me beyond words. His tormented face appeared, and I could not run away fast enough. It was funny how things changed. Instead of running away from the young man, I would run straight into his arms—if given the chance.

The old, warped door to the basement was latched. That tiny, brass hook was all that sealed off the dreaded space beneath my feet. As much as I feared it, there was no better place to find answers. There was no place as dark and there was no place as deep. If Adalynn had something to hide, it would be in that basement.

I put the cleaning supplies down and gathered my hair over one shoulder. With a flick of a finger, the latch was off. "Easy enough,"

I told myself. Then, my eyes locked onto the brass knob. It glared back, daring me to turn it. Before losing the nerve, I took it in my hand, turned and pushed, all in one swift motion.

With a grating screech, the door swung into the shadows. I held my breath, bit back my fears, and reluctantly reached into the darkness. My hand felt along the wall, but the light switches were just beyond my reach. I stretched out and strained my shaking arm to find them. Then with a *click, click, click, click* and the buzzing hum of electricity, the room below brightened in succession.

I exhaled with relief and shook off my trembling hands. "It's just a room," I tried to convince myself, but my voice wavered and a lump swelled in my throat.

The old wooden stairs creaked and cracked under the soles of my moccasins. I stifled a sneeze with one hand while dodging cobwebs with the other. The moment my feet left the bottom step, a damp chill clung to my skin. I shrunk down into my shoulders and hugged myself for comfort and warmth.

The basement was *almost* a friendlier place, brightened with incandescent bulbs rather than by candlelight. Unfortunately, that was not saying very much. Although the space was large, it was cluttered and claustrophobic. Cardboard boxes were stacked in tall, lopsided towers, and were marked with a faded stamp from the mill. Rows of metal shelves were bolted along the length of the jagged, limestone walls. They were stocked with rusty tools and out-dated supplies. The room had low ceilings and a floor made of hard-packed dirt and more rough-cut stone. The air smelled of mildew and a thick blanket of dust coated everything in sight. That basement, and all that was in it, was simply left to rot away.

With a tight grip on the hem of my blouse, I crept through the maze of damp cardboard boxes. Even with my neck craned while standing on my toes, I could barely see over them. Something was hidden in the far corner, but there were too many boxes in the way to make it out. With a steady shove of the hip, I moved a few stacks aside and found a metal crib and basinet stowed against the back wall. I pushed another tower of cardboard aside and jolted back in fear. Two glossy eyes peered at me from the shadows! My heart hammered like a drum in my chest. Then, I saw the antique doll more clearly. It was swaddled and tucked inside an old wicker stroller. I laughed and then stood there, silently staring at its sunken eyes. They seemed to flicker in the sockets as the doll mocked me with a demented little smile. My skin crawled as the creeps set in. I slowly backed away and stumbled when my heel hit something from behind.

Resting amongst the other boxes was a vintage alligator-skin suitcase. I sat cross-legged on the floor and unhooked the lid. As the case screeched open, dust sprinkled down onto a stack of paper. On the very top was a medical record written in a swift but fine hand. It was the diagnoses of a ten-year-old Adalynn King in 1945, the year World War II ended and the year Evelyn King found her daughter on the riverbank. The examination confirmed that Adalynn was in perfect physical condition and showed no injuries. The physician concluded that she suffered from shock and mental fatigue caused by the near drowning.

I placed the delicate pages on the floor and delved back into the suitcase. There were more medical records with a letterhead belonging to a Dr. H. Dubois. The papers detailed a series of psychiatric evaluations, dated 1946. The doctor wrote that eleven-year-old Adalynn King was disturbed. Her refusal to speak, read, and write was a direct result of having a traumatic near-death experience. Apparently, when she returned to school, Adalynn responded with severe displays of hysteria. Her reactions were so extreme that she needed to be physically restrained. The last assessment ended with Dr. Dubois' final recommendation.

"If the child's erratic behavior continues, it will be in her best interest to receive professional care at home or be institutionalized."

An unpleasant chill passed through my body upon reading the austere statement. With a furrowed brow, I put the medical papers aside. An unopened package from *The Institute for the Deaf-Mute Society* lay just beneath them. Inside, there was an official letter from the dean, welcoming Miss Adalynn King to the school. There was also a course booklet and an extensive application form that was never filled out.

At the bottom of the suitcase were some old snapshots of Adalynn in various stages of her life. One picture captured a callous woman wearing a white pinafore apron and cap. Her hands rested heavily on Adalynn's shoulders. All the other pictures were very much the same. In every snapshot, Adalynn's expression was grim, with a new nurse standing by her side. Seeing young Adalynn so unhappy made my heart ache. My eyes clouded over with tears. No wonder the suitcase was left to rot in the basement of Kingsgrove.

I was about to snap the lid shut for good when something unexpected stopped me. Like a tiny jewel at the bottom of a hopeless pile of hardship, another picture appeared. This picture was very different from the rest. I held it in my hand and felt the heartache fade away. The petite nurse standing next to Miss King had a toothy smile that no one would ever forget. I recognised it right away, and sure enough, written on the back was *Jo-Anne Peters, 1973*. JoJo wore a white knee-length dress with a matching cap nested in curls. The beautiful Adalynn was next to her, looking sophisticated and wonderfully vintage. She wore gossamer from head to toe with her long wavy hair parted down the middle. I gazed through teary eyes and smiled. JoJo had been around for over twenty years! It was the only photo in the suitcase where Adalynn actually looked happy.

I sat quietly as medical jargon and water-stained photos whirled around in my head. All the *what ifs* and *could have beens* consumed my thoughts. If not for JoJo, Adalynn would have been at the mercy of one apathetic nurse after another. That or worse—her parents could have sent her away to grow up in a mental institution! The thought sickened me. She was not crazy—eccentric, yes, but not crazy. In fact, she was quite capable. If she were disturbed, JoJo certainly would not have hired a person like me—a person with no professional experience or credentials. I was only there to maintain the estate and keep its mistress company. No, JoJo did not think Adalynn was crazy. Even she was more of a friend then a nurse. I had seen them together, and the way JoJo went on while . . . *tap* . . . *tap* . . . *tap* . . .

What was that?

Tap . . . tap . . . tap . . .

It was right behind me.

Tap . . . tap . . . tap . . .

My back stiffened as I froze with fear. Was it blood dripping from the hem of a nightgown? Did the gruesome phantom return to attack me?

Tap . . . tap . . . tap . . .

My heart pumped and pounded brutally in my chest. Ever so slowly, I stood up with my back still facing the ominous sound.

Time stood still as I held my breath and turned around.

SAINTS AND SINS

The sound of dripping blood echoed off the limestone walls. I was not alone.

Tap . . . tap . . . tap . . .

My eardrums throbbed with every heartbeat, and my vision blurred. Consumed by fear, I turned to face the phantom woman and saw . . . a leaky pipe.

I gripped a fistful of my hair at the scalp and released a trembling exhale. Without hesitating, I soared up the stairs and lunged into the hallway. To stop myself from collapsing, I searched for something solid to hold onto. With a stumble, my body found the wall across from the basement door. My face rested on the plaster finish, which cooled my blood-drained cheek. With my eyes closed, I focused on the hard surface as it pressed against my heaving chest. The building held me up as it tried to push me down. The irony was not lost on me.

Eventually, I stepped away from the wall and turned off the basement lights. With the brass latch, I sealed the door then left the narrow corridor. The silver locket swung at my neck as my arms strained to pull the broom and cleaners up the stairs. How I managed to find the strength to go on, was beyond me. I was constantly being challenged and repressed. It was hard to imagine why the ghost called me the *white hawk*. It sounded so glorious and strong. I wanted to embody that, but doubt still teased my mind like little whispered promises of defeat. Instinctually, I knew something was coming—something bad. My gut was screaming for me to run away from Willow Vale and never look back. Instead of listening, I continued up the stairway and went deeper into bowel of Kingsgrove.

Straightaway, I went to work, wiping down and sweeping out the hallways that crisscrossed within the large estate. I dragged the broom along the baseboards and hummed softy to kill the silence. Out of nowhere, the grandfather clock chimed bright and loud. My heart practically leapt from my chest in surprise. The clock was only a few feet away, cast in shadow, at the end of the eastern corridor. I walked over and watched it tick the time away. Forever constant and uncaring, it swung its pendulum and stole another second of our lives.

I broke free from the clock's hypnotic grip and turned toward a set of large double doors. Behind the towering oak entryway was the master bedroom. The room that once belonged to Jonathan and Evelyn King felt so private and closed off, I had not dared to enter it before.

Would it be *so bad* to go in? I wondered. Miss King was still knitting on the veranda. What she did not know wouldn't hurt her. Right?

I needed to find answers, wherever they may be. After all, Adalynn was not about to speak the hidden truths she locked deep inside. Before losing the nerve, I grabbed both handles, clenched my jaw, and pushed on the heavy doors—they swung open to a massive room buried in darkness. The gloomy daylight barely peeked from behind the lush curtains hanging in the windows.

At the flip of a switch, a glorious chandelier came to life at the center of the vaulted ceiling. Its brilliance surpassed the dusty cobwebs that wilted off each glowing tier. The dripping crystals refracted light throughout, apart from one area of the room. The chandelier did nothing to brighten the deepest corner where a four-poster bed stood draped in blue velvet. My skin tingled with dread as

I peered at the shrouded frame. To my knowledge, no one had slept in there for years. Despite that, its grand, concealed presence gave me the most uneasy feeling. In apprehension, I took a step back. With fear in my eyes, I stared longingly down the hallway, then back to the master bedroom.

My mind spiraled with indecision, that was, until I thought of the ghost. On the first night he appeared, the young man said, *You need to look around you. All the answers are there.*

The clouded memory gave me bit of hope. "All the answers are there." I muttered his words then stepped back into the bedroom. With resolve, I pulled the doors closed and hid myself inside.

The air in the room was stagnant and the smoky odor of cigar, though faint, was hard to miss. I thought little of it and crept across the room, cringing as the floorboards creaked underfoot. Wasting no time at all, I searched through every dresser drawer and cabinet. Except for some old clothes, folded away and left to the moths, they were empty. I noticed a steamer trunk and rooted through it only to find vintage boots and high heels inside. Even the collection of hat boxes in the corner held only the hats they were fashioned for. I knew this, because I lifted every lid to see each delicate headpiece. They were all quite special, though one stood out amongst the rest. It was small and adorned with white feathers and lace. For a short time, my fears were forgotten as I pinned the hat to my hair.

It was like a dream to be amidst all of Evelyn's things. In a whimsical daze, I sat at her gilded vanity. An array of frosted glass perfume bottles and powders were set out before me. A matching comb, brush, and hand-mirror were placed perfectly in a row. Lips pursed, I blew the dust away to reveal the inlays of shell and pearl. Through the tumbling flecks, I saw myself in the vanity's bevelled mirror. Instead of an elegant mill owner's wife, there was a tired girl in the reflection. Like the falling rain outside, I was brought back to earth. Reality set in, and I pulled the white hat out of my hair.

The daydream was gone and my focus went to the room behind me, reflecting in the mirror.

Opposite the vanity was a grand fireplace guarded by a pair of regal lions. The ceramic statues were fiercely posed with wild manes and their fangs exposed. I got up from the vanity to cross the room and knelt by the open hearth. Pools of hardened wax were spattered on the cut-stone surface, as if someone had burned candles there instead of wood. I brushed aside the silken cobwebs and shifted my body to see up the chimney. A faint whistle of misty wind resonated through the flue. The chilly air swept along my neck, pouring shivers down my spine. With my shirt pulled more tightly around me, I bit my bottom lip, then reached up inside. My hand was shaking as it felt for anything that might be tucked into the cracks. I soon found the only thing hiding in the fireplace was a nest of frightened spiders. One dropped down and scurried across my hand. I jerked back and wacked it to the ground. In the blink of an eye, the tiny eight-legged creature disappeared in a gap between the floorboards.

With a sigh, I wiped my ashy palms on my pants then turned back to face the room. Positioned in front of fireplace was a club chair and chaise lounge. On hands and knees, I crawled over to look under them. Again, there was nothing. I stayed low and shuffled along to see under the other furniture. My knees bit into the floor while moving around the room. Before long, I was kneeling next to the bed. I craned my neck to look up at the dusty, velvet covering. It loomed over and made my nerves prickle from head to toe. Unfortunately, there was only one place left uncovered—only one place left unexplored.

Gingerly, I lifted the bed skirt. Without a light, it was difficult to see anything under the king-sized bed. Irritated with myself for forgetting to buy a flashlight, I lay on my stomach for a better angle. My eyes strained to penetrate the mote-filled shadows, then a smile curled at the corner of my lips. It was hard to make out, but something was there, pushed deep into the dark. I could just barely see the edge of what appeared to be a box. All I had to do was reach in and grab for it.

I hesitated.

It was foolish to think that the little girl in me was gone forever. Her broken innocence haunted me at every turn. Kingsgrove had a way of dragging her out to expose my utmost vulnerabilities. As I lay there, the childhood fear of monsters waiting to strike from under the bed gnawed at my memory. Except the monsters that afflicted my youth were imaginary, and the monsters of Kingsgrove were very, very real.

I balled my hand into a tight fist and gently bit a knuckle. Leaving the box behind would haunt me. I knew there was no turning back. Curiosity had overpowered the fear tugging at my instincts. Before all courage was lost, I decided to throw caution to the wind.

"Here we go," I said breathlessly, opening my fist and reaching into the dark.

My heart palpitated as I struggled to find the box with my out-stretched hand. Infected with anxiety and frustration, my entire body shuddered and shook. After clawing away unsuccessfully for what seemed like forever, I finally reached the box. My fingertips fumbled helplessly with its frayed, leather handle. "Thank you!" I rejoiced when they finally hooked around it. With a firm hold and an awkward pull, the box slid out from under the bed.

I sat cross-legged on the floor before my newest discovery. It was a military footlocker, painted drab green with a faded insignia stenciled on the top. I ran my hand over the golden wings, unfurled aside a red and white star. My guess was Air force, maybe World War II era. Unfortunately, whom it belonged to still remained a mystery. Throughout Kingsgrove, there were no pictures of anyone in uniform. Plus, there was no mention of any Kings ever being enlisted. It seemed so out of place. So much so, that the suspense was killing me.

What was in the box?

I pried at the stiff metal latches and they flipped up with a loud snap, making me flinch. With a firm grip, I lifted the heavy lid. Part of me expected it to be an empty, forgotten box, and part of me expected it to be a time capsule of military relics—it was neither. Instead, it was exactly what I had been looking for.

The search was over. I had my answer. Adalynn was practicing Voodoo, and it was more than a sprinkle of salt to ward off unpleasant things. She was not just a fearful woman playing around with meager superstitions. The footlocker held a variety of items separated by the different compartments. There were all sorts of ritualistic bits and pieces of the strange magic, though nothing looked particularly dark or evil. It was entirely unlike the charms that hung from the trees outside Scarlet Eventide's cabin.

Without touching a thing, I examined each oddity sectioned out before me. A plaster statue of Saint Peter laid there, all chipped and crackled with age. My grandmother was catholic. I recognized him instantly, as his tiny hand held tight to the golden key. The *guardian of the gate* was next to an assortment of roots and herbs, bound with string and a stark white feather. Vials of oil and sticks of incense were unmarked and stored with care. A mickey of rum and a snubbed-out cigar were placed side-by-side in their own compartment. That explained the smoky smell in the room—the entire box stunk of it.

There was also a set of three black and white tapered candles, wrapped in cloth. I thought of the melted wax in the fireplace and quickly made the connection. Little pieces of the puzzle were finally coming together. Even a rosary made of cowry shells reminded me of the colorful jewellery worn by Ruby Monrose. Then it dawned on me. Did the librarian practice Voodoo as well?

I remember her necklace—the silver octagon of spears—the very same emblem carved into Adalynn's rowboat.

It had to be true!

There was more to Miss Monrose than the unassuming book-worm who hid between the stacks of the public library. For some reason, it made perfect sense. I needed it to make sense. I needed it to be true. While helping to translate the Latin chant, Ruby could tell me more about Voodoo. After all, she did say to come to her if I needed help.

Wait. Why *did* she say that? Once I thought about it, her offer was kind of out of nowhere and a little strange. Did she know something? Could she be trusted?

Before exposing too much, I had to make sure Ruby's intentions were sincere. It was likely that Voodoo had both a good and evil purpose. If she was using it for good, then it was time to call in a favor.

While I sat by the bed lost in thought, the fireplace whistled from the wind and the temperature in the room plummeted. At that exact moment, an odd sensation came over me. It felt like a static pull from above was lifting my hair. Before I could react, my scalp erupted with pain! Someone had grabbed a fistful of my hair and was pulling me through the velvet drapes! My screams were deafening! My limbs thrashed while the attacker dragged me into the shrouded bed.

It was pitch-black.

Then, just as fast as it began, it ended. For a fleeting moment, nothing happened.

I lay there paralyzed, only hearing my own frantic gasps for breath. Just when I thought it might be over, the entity lunged at me! The hit was like a blast of frozen steal, slamming against my chest! I cried as the wind was bashed out of my lungs. My spine curled in agony and my hands grasped at my heaving stomach. Ghostly laughter lilted into the air, followed by a low, demonic growl. Before I could catch my breath, the entity came at me again. There was no escaping it—*it* moved too quickly. In a split second, I was pinned on my back. Two cold hands clutched the sides of my face, icy fingers splayed across my cheeks. It shook my head brutally and bashed it against the mattress. My neck burned as the muscles and tendons were wrenched and twisted.

Time seemed to slow down and speed up all at once. It was what I always imagined an out-of-body experience would be like. If not for the pain, I would have thought I was already dead. Even my screams came from a place within me that I did not know existed. Each cry that escaped my lips was torn from the very depth of my soul. The shrieking sound sliced through the dense air inside the velvet drapes.

It was no use. My screams were pointless. There was no one to hear them—no one to rescue me. Plus, my opponent seemed to feed off the terror and was only getting stronger! *It* hit me again and again, each strike scorching my skin. The pain was unbearably sharp, but I refused to give up. Adrenaline gushed through my veins as I swung blindly in the direction of my attacker. Each time my fists made contact, electricity surged up my arm. The shock coursed through my system and stung me to the bone.

Clearly, this *thing* wanted me dead. *It* wrestled me viscously and violently, desperate to keep the upper hand. Scratches seared down my arms and stomach. I cried out in agony. It was like battling a rabid animal with a serious thirst for blood.

The more we fought the angrier I felt. This *thing* was trying to stop me! I was closing in on the truth! I was on the right path, and *it* was afraid.

The realization was empowering, and I refused to be the victim again. The anger boiled up inside me. With every last bit of my strength, I reached out. My hands burned, so I knew the attacker was in my grasp. Through gritted teeth, I yelled with all my might and threw the entity off!

For a spit second, I was free! It was my chance to escape.

Just as I gripped onto the drapes, the icy hands locked around my ankles. The shock paralyzed my system and a torrent of pain shot up my legs. The hands yanked me back, but I did not let go. I was able to twist around and use the momentum to pull at the heavy velvet.

Light saturated the bed.

For a moment, I almost wished for the darkness to return. My mind could hardly believe what my eyes were seeing. Crouched at my feet was the spirit of the young woman. Her feral eyes glistened, like two glassy, black spheres. Like an insect, she blinked and twitched her disjointed, wiry frame.

It was horrifying.

Thankfully, the sudden, invasive light stunned the phantom and she released my ankles. She crept back, bared her teeth, and hissed. We locked eyes . . . then, out of pure instinct, I kicked her—I kicked her hard! The blow sent her flying backward, vanishing through the drapes. Chest heaving for air, I crawled over to look out at the room. The woman was gone. Flakes of dust snowed over me as I knelt on the edge.

My mind went blank in shock.

What just happened? Did I just fight a ghost? Did I win? I had won! Wait . . . I won?

My head spun with euphoria and shock. The violent encounter left me in a daze. The last thing I remembered was smiling as the room went dark. Victory was mine. Little did I know, the battle had just begun.

✗ ✗ ✗

A dull headache woke me from a deep sleep. Sun poured into the room and spilled onto the bed. I shielded my blurry eyes from the blinding light. The white curtains billowed into the room, carrying a summer breeze that revived the stale air.

I felt misplaced and twisted around. It was not my room.

Did I fall asleep in Jonathan and Evelyn's bed? No, it was not their bed at all. It was smaller and there was no velvet draped between the four posters. I blinked until my vision cleared. It took a moment for me to recognize the room—the empty room in the west wing. The one with the picture-less frames hanging on the walls. The room that felt so lonely and forgotten.

How did I end up there, tucked between the musty sheets?

The last thing I remembered was fighting the ghastly female spirit. I went to run a hand through my tangled hair and winced. My scalp was tender from the woman's clawing grasp, and the damage did not end there. Eyes wide in shock, I saw my arms for the first time and a whimper caught in my throat. Angry red scratches marred my freckled skin. Frantically, I rubbed my arms as if it would make them disappear, but the welted marks stayed. They lingered and burned like my hatred for the phantom woman.

At least I managed to fight back. At least she knew I would not give up easily.

Was it possible that I actually had a fighting chance? I held the silver locket in my fist and felt the chain pull at my neck. Was I stronger than I thought?

I let the locket fall against my chest and wondered once again how I ended up in that lonely room. I should have been frightened, but I was not—I felt safe. Something told me the young man had brought me there. Perhaps it was how the rain had stopped and the sun shone through the open window.

When I found a gift resting next to me on the sheets, I knew it had to be true. It was a freshly picked, white magnolia. Ever so gently, I took it in my hand and inhaled its creamy, sweet scent. A flower from my ghost; I would cherish it forever.

THIS IS VOODOO

Night had arrived and a tranquil moon rose in the blackened sky. A fusion of classic jazz spun on the old record player in the east parlor. Adalynn was teaching me to crochet with great patience while I chatted about the mundane, leaving out the messy details of my fearful situation. Spending these quiet moments with Miss King helped to reign in my sanity. In so little time, my world had been torn apart and twisted. I was caught in a whirlwind of dark secrets and ghostly attacks. Some may call it tenacity, but I knew it was my hard-headed, stubborn nature forcing on a brave face. I tried my best to hide the fear, though Adalynn knew I was haunted. No words were needed to show her concern; it was written in every tender glance—in every gentle touch of her hand.

By the time I crocheted a small white doily, we were yawning together in chorus. Adalynn smiled kindly as I laughed at my misshaped masterpiece. I wiped a sleepy tear from my eye and sighed. For a moment, the stress melted away, only to return in an instant. All the ghosts, spells, and of course Voodoo weighed me down, like a load-full of loose ends and unanswered questions.

To make matters worse, the *Backwater Summer Fair* was scheduled to start in a day. According to the front-page article of the *Willow Vale Gazette*, it was the pride of Willow Vale. The population would double and the streets would be fortified with festive lights and streamers. It meant all the businesses and shops would close their doors for the entire weekend, including the *Willow Vale Public Library*. There was only one day left until the town was completely shut down. My window of opportunity was about to close. There was no time to waste. The next morning, I would return to the library and have a face-to-face with Ruby Monrose.

✘ ✘ ✘

Gust after gust of wind and rain spattered against my window. I looked beyond the water-blurred panes at the leaden sky. The morning sun hid behind another miserable day, and it was more than a passing, summer shower. A thunderstorm thrashed its way through backwoods and ravaged the small, southern town. Lights dimmed and the estate rumbled with every stroke of lightning. The atmosphere was alive with the fallout of nature's power.

With anticipation, I waited to see if the young man would appear, but he did not. Still, a pleasant shiver trickled along my skin. The gentle hum of his energy surrounded me like a cool embrace, turning my cheeks an embarrassing shade of pink.

"I met a lady the other day that might be able to help," I said. "Her name is Ruby. She's my only hope. So . . . cross your fingers."

The ghost offered no reply.

I stared at the floor, absently twirling a strand of my hair. In the quietest of whispers, I added, "I miss you." My heart ached as my sincere words dangled in the air. The emotions budding inside me were uncharted. That part of me seemed nonexistent before the ghost. It was all too new and exposing. Self-consciously, I turned and left, but not without looking back until the room shrunk away in the dark.

Down in the kitchen, Adalynn was percolating coffee while gazing out the window. Lost in thought, she hadn't noticed me enter the room.

"Good morning." Adalynn jumped at the sound of my voice. "Sorry I startled you." I chuckled and looked inside the fridge. "We need some more food, don't you think, Miss King?" I turned back to face her.

With concern, she gestured toward the window at the storm. The wind threw the rain at an alarming angle.

I smiled sweetly to put her at ease. "I'm not worried, Ada." I pointed at the newspaper on the table. "The forecast says the storm will pass."

It was a lie. Adalynn saw right through it and scowled disapprovingly.

We regarded each other for a moment, a stubborn smile fixed to my face. "It'll be fine. I promise. It's important that I go . . . to get groceries. We need them." My tone implied an ulterior motive. Eyes narrowed, she handed me a steaming cup of black coffee.

Adalynn seemed to get the hint, and just like that, it was settled. Storm or no storm, it was time to get help—some help in the form of a pocket-sized librarian.

I downed my coffee and grabbed a muffin for the road. With only one foot out the door, it became clear why Miss King was so concerned. The storm raged and roared, whipping my hair around like white flames in the wind. I gathered the flying strands and tucked them under the hood of my sweatshirt. With car keys in hand, I left the safety of the veranda and ran out into the rain. The Trans Am was only a few strides away; still, my clothes were soaked before the key was in the ignition.

It was a slow, wary drive down the muddy lane. I prayed silently for the path to be clear. If the marsh flooded over, my trip would be over before it even began. Thankfully, my car managed to crawl along the road, out to the suburban streets of Willow Vale. Kings Lane was not washed out . . . yet.

I tried to ignore the anxiety turning in my stomach. In truth, the newspaper affirmed the storm would rage on until nightfall. It certainly showed no signs of passing. The road would likely flood, but it was an obstacle I had to face when the time came. There was enough to worry about already. Assuming Ruby was even at the library, there was still a lingering question that needed answering—could she be trusted?

I knew nothing about Voodoo and its purpose. If my theories were correct, and she did meddle with the strange magic, would she even help me? I had to choose my words carefully and reveal only what was necessary. Hopefully, my prying would come across as a mild curiosity. As for the Latin chant, there was no way to bring it up without arousing some suspicion. Nevertheless, I was tired of being lost somewhere between normal and arcane while balancing on the edge of life and death. Risk or no risk, there was no stopping me. I was in too deep.

As the Trans Am rumbled at the corner of Main and LiGrand, nerves pinched my stomach. The windshield wipers swung back and forth, revealing the public library through the watery glass. I parked then reluctantly left my dry car behind to sprint toward the front steps. Out of breath and soaked to the bone, I pulled on the heavy front doors—but they resisted. My heart sank. The building was sealed up and locked tight. I peered through the narrow glass to see the towering stacks were blanketed in darkness. With force, I shook the handles again. Exasperated, I slid my back down the door until my bottom hit the cement stoop. All the hope inside me seeped away in an instant. Head tilted back, I closed my eyes and surrendered to the rain. The warm drops washed over my crestfallen face.

There was no plan B.

Crushed and feeling sorry for myself, I sat there for a while, wallowing in disappointment. Of course the library would close for one of Willow Vale's gale-force storms.

What was I thinking!

"Miss Wyld?!" The sound of Ruby's voice rang through the downpour. A rush of pure relief made my heart jump for joy. I rubbed the water from my face to look up at her. The tiny librarian hid under a polka-dot umbrella that looked like it could easily swallow her whole.

I smiled sheepishly, squinting against the onslaught of rain. Ruby was completely bewildered by the sight of me. "Are you okay?" she asked.

"Yes. I'm sorry. This must seem very strange, that I'm sitting here in the rain." I stood up and stammered on. "It's just that . . . I was hoping the library was open, and it clearly isn't. You see, I need some . . . information. Well actually, I was hoping to come speak with you. To, ah . . . get some help with the information that I need." My voice trailed off. It was painfully awkward.

Miss Monrose regarded me with a confused tilt of the head. "Come with me, Emilie," she said finally, pulling me under her umbrella. "First, we get you dry and warm. Then, we talk. Okay *cherie*?"

To my surprise, Ruby did not take me into the library. She guided me to an alleyway that ran behind the building. As we rounded the corner, lightning lit the sky, sending a crash of thunder in its wake. We both stopped and looked up until the rumble passed. While huddled together, I smelled the heady scent of patchouli in her curly hair.

"This way," Ruby murmured. We linked arms to stay close and continued on.

The alleyway came to a path that brought us to a little house effectively hidden by a massive willow tree. Ruby took my hand and lured me through the veil of weeping branches. After leaving her umbrella on the front step, she pulled me out of the rain into the warm glow of her house. The spicy scent of incense tickled my nose as the door closed behind me. Ruby kicked off her sandals and I did the same.

Through a beaded curtain, we entered the front room, which was colorfully decorated with the exotic and obscure. All the sights and smells overwhelmed my senses. Before I had a chance to soak it all in, Ruby turned to face me. "I'll be right back. Make yourself at home, Emilie." Like a mouse, she scampered out of the room.

With Ruby gone, I was able to take in my surroundings. The room was cluttered, but not messy. It was draped and dressed with a kaleidoscope of tapestries and vibrant materials. There was a small vintage settee and a coffee table filled with burning candles and mysterious curios. A corner fireplace, nearly half the size of those at Kingsgrove, caught my eye. The mantel was laden with a ceremonial-type alter. Tentatively, I walked over. An old religious figurine stood in the center. The female saint was unfamiliar to me. She wore a pink and white robe, trimmed in gold, with a crown of roses on her head. An anchor rested at her side, and she held an arrow and a sprig of ivy in her hand. Offerings of perfume and dried flowers were laid out and blue candles burned all around. A large cockleshell holding a charred bundle of sage spilled ashes at her feet. There was so much to see, yet I could not look away from the catholic figurine. The paint-chipped face was so gentle and young. I was dazzled by its virtue.

"She is Mambo Filomèz." I turned to find Ruby standing behind me. She was looking up at the statue in reverence. In her sweet Creole accent, she went on. "The Catholics name her Saint Philomena; a young martyr that died to keep her purity. I call on her spirit for good fortune, strength, and love. "This," Ruby gestured to the offerings, "is a gift to Filomèz, so I can receive her favor."

"You're not Catholic?" I wondered.

She shook her head with a little smile. "No *cherie*. This is Voodoo."

Our eyes locked.

It was true! Ruby Monrose practiced Voodoo. She practiced Voodoo just like Scarlet Eventide and just like the mistress of Kingsgrove. She looked up at me, seemingly expecting a reaction. I waited for the fear to come, but my intuition was at ease.

I felt safe.

"But these figures are Catholic saints." I was so confused.

"Willow Vale is home to all kinds of people, from all over. They come from the north, the south, the east, and the west. They brought with them their gods, saints, and even demons. Voodoo is a free-form method of worship. Those who practice, work with these spirits to bring about change in their lives."

I nodded in understanding as Ruby handed me a towel. I took it gratefully. "You should change out of these wet clothes, Miss Wyld. You will be meeting with the Ghede Nibo if you do not." She saw the confused look on my face and clarified. "The God of the dead."

I shivered and took the t-shirt that Ruby offered without argument. We turned away from each other as I peeled off my wet shirt, and put on her dry one. The soft cotton felt so nice against my damp, cool skin. The logo on the front read, *Laveau Nightclub* in blood-red script.

We turned to face each other again. Before the conversation changed course, I remembered the religious statue hidden inside the footlocker. "Say someone was to call upon the spirit of Saint Peter, what sort of favors would that someone be asking for?"

"Ah, this is Papa Legba. He is a very important spirit. He stands at the crossroads between this world and the next." Ruby brought me over to the entryway. She pointed up to a card wedged into the doorframe depicting the image of Saint Peter. "If you acknowledge him, he will allow you to pass peacefully into the spiritual world when you die. If you invoke him, you wish to gain access for yourself or someone else. I burn a yellow candle every night for Papa Legba."

It took a moment for the new information to sink in. If the footlocker belonged to Adalynn, then she had been calling on Papa Legba. Perhaps it was an attempt to help the young man gain access to the spiritual world. Perhaps she was trying to move him on. Either way, it had not worked. He was still neither here nor there; he was trapped somewhere between.

"What about Voodoo dolls?" I blurted. Since seeing them on display at *The Eventide Emporium*, I had been curious.

"Poppets," she corrected me. "Poppets are used for different reasons. They can be made with sticks, bound with cotton. This cotton is stuffed with herbs and other elements depending on your intention. Concealing an item like hair, blood, or a piece of clothing will directly link the poppet to your target. With help from the spirits, you must perform a naming ritual to fuse the connection. Once the ritual is complete, you hide your poppet to prevent discovery. If the poppet is found, the magic can be removed or avenged."

"Are they used for curses?" I wondered.

"Yes, Emilie. Poppets are used to aid, hex, or seek revenge."

My mind was swimming. I was thoroughly captivated by the organic, yet unearthly culture. Since coming to Willow Vale, my eyes had been opened. I could see for the first time.

Ghosts did exist . . . and so did magic.

"Is this the information you seek, Emilie?" She had a knowing smile on her pretty little face.

"Yes." The answer was simple, but there was still more questions to be asked. "In Voodoo rituals, is there chanting?"

"There can be," she replied.

"Would these chants be in another language, like Latin?" I pressed.

Ruby's eyes narrowed ever so slightly. "The songs I sing are in English and Creole. Latin is most often used in the dark arts or the left-handed path. You can choose to mix this with Voodoo. However, it is very dangerous. Evil magic is a sweet mistress. With sacrifice, you can gain great power. This is something I do not seek."

A crack of thunder shook the tiny house. All of the candle flames danced with the sudden blast. I was startled by the sound as it interrupted our dark conversation. Even Ruby's lighthearted demeanor had turned grave and serious.

Despite the change in atmosphere, I had to go on. "Do you understand Latin, Ruby? I need to have something translated."

"I know a little. Here . . . take this." She handed me a pencil and pad of paper from the coffee table. "Write it down. Do not speak this Latin out loud." We sat next to each other on the settee. Carefully, I printed the mantra.

Concede mortem ad cubiculum, obscuro infinitum. Pueri spiritus redeat ad corpus.

The foreign words were laced into my memory forever. They flowed through my body, out of my hand, and onto the paper. Ruby put on her glasses and took the written mantra into her hands. She bit her bottom lip and studied it quietly. I held my breath as the librarian reached for the pencil and wrote below the Latin chant. When finished, she handed the paper back to me. The words seemed to pulse on the page as I stared down at them.

Yield to the death chamber, the dark infinity. Child's spirit returns to the body.

"Where did you hear this, Emilie?" Ruby's voice was small and guarded.

"In a dream." It was not a lie. It was not the whole truth either.

"This is a spell. A very powerful one. Have you heard of necromancy?"

I shook my head *no*.

"It is magic that brings life back to the dead. This is not natural. If you do this, there must be a trade. With magic like this, there must be sacrifice. There *must* be balance."

Thunder roared outside again, making us both jump in our seats. As a reaction, Ruby grabbed my arm. The rumbling passed, but she did not let go. Instead, she looked down at my arm in horror. My heart pounded wildly once I realized what she saw. The angry scratches inflicted by the phantom woman still marked my skin.

"What is going on, Emilie? Where did you get these?" She looked at me over the rims her glasses. I could see the concern in her almond eyes.

"Miss King has a cat," I lied a little too quickly, pulling my arm away and rubbing it. "I tried to stop it from clawing the furniture and it turned on me." Ruby eyed me suspiciously as I got up from the settee. With a stiff smile, I gathered my wet clothes. The conversation was hanging dangerously on the edge of truth. If I stayed any longer, she would learn too much. Trustworthy or not, Ruby would suggest a padded room if she knew I was seeing ghosts.

It was time to leave. "Thank you for all your help, Miss Monrose. I really should be heading back to Kingsgrove."

"Just one moment." Ruby stopped me as I headed for the door. "I have something for you." She went over to a chest of drawers across the room. It was littered with an array of curiosities, botanical powders, and bottled oils. She took a small red flannel sack, then named off some strange components as she filled it. "A broken length of chain, a rat's bone, a cats-eye shell, five-finger grass, a nail, a pinch of salt and . . ." Ruby turned to me, presenting a small pair of scissors. Instinctually, I leaned away as she snipped a lock of my ashen hair, which she also added to the bag. With a leather cord, it was sealed. Ruby passed the sack through the flame of a blue candle then anointed the sack with a sprinkle of oil before handing it over. "This is a gris-gris bag. It will protect you. Keep it close."

"Thank you." For some reason my heart swelled at the strange but kind gift.

"Remember, Emilie. I'm always here to lend a hand," Ruby stressed. "*Bonne chance, cherie.*"

With gris-gris bag in hand, I said goodbye and then left the small house hidden in the willows.

THE VULTURES' DANCE

The streets of Willow Vale were empty. I was the only person crazy enough to venture out that stormy day. Without wasting any time, I turned down Kings Lane to head home. The Trans Am slipped precariously on the mucky road. It slid and swerved all the way until arriving at an impasse. As suspected, the rain prevailed. The rising water in the everglades drowned the road ahead. Whatever glimmer of hope I was holding onto had slipped away. Any sane person with a bit of common sense would have just stayed home. At that moment, it was fair to say that I was pretty unhinged. Instead of listening to my head, I was listening to my heart, and as far as *it* was concerned, the voice of reason was hardly a whisper—so easy to ignore.

My car idled on the edge of the hopeless situation. The flooded hollow was too deep. My old Trans Am would never make it out alive. It seemed that the only way home was to walk. There was roughly two miles of marshy forest between my car and Kingsgrove. Giving in, I turned the key, and the engine sputtered to a stop.

Thunder still rumbled somewhere in the distance, but for the moment, the storm had eased into a steady rainfall. I struggled back into my damp sweatshirt and stepped out of the car, cringing when my feet sunk into the ground. There was no choice but to kiss my flip-flops goodbye, as they burrowed beep into the mud. Sadly, this was the least of my worries. The water spilled across the road, making it impossible to pass at either side. Barefoot and determined, I rolled my pants and waded through the mucky, brown pool. It was deeper than I expected. Even on my tippy toes, the water crept up until my jeans were soaked to the knee.

I made it out the other side and began the more-than-unpleasant walk home. With only a gloomy sky to light the way, my skin was crawling. The forest was deathly still. My footsteps echoed with the patter of rain, as if the shadows themselves mimicked my every move. I glanced back more than once, thinking someone was there, creeping up from behind.

Trying to ignore the pang of anxiety, I recounted my visit with Ruby Monrose. The librarian had given me quite a bit to think about. With open arms, she invited me into her world and I entered willingly, knowing there was no coming back.

Nothing was truly black and white. Reality was skewed like the funhouse mirrors in a never-ending carnival, forever distorting what you thought to be true. And there I was, returning to Kingsgrove at the heart of all the chaos. Fortunately, I left Ruby's home enlightened, more or less. Bits and pieces of the mystery were cast in a new light. For instance, I knew Adalynn practiced Voodoo, though not to what extent. Obviously, she did not delve as deep as Miss Monrose. She merely flirted with the local folklore and superstitions. The military footlocker held only a few ritualistic elements. It was not nearly as stocked as Ruby's chest of drawers. Either way, there was no need to worry about Ruby Monrose or Adalynn and their strange magic. I was convinced their version of Voodoo was, no matter how extraordinary, meant for *good*.

It appeared that Willow Vale was crawling with the *spiritual* and *superstitious*. That included the Eventides, of course. There was no way to tell how the family of women, living and dead, were connected to Kingsgrove and its ghosts. Only one thing was for sure— they wanted to keep outsiders away from their cabin, at all costs.

That alone led me to believe there was more to the Eventides than it may have seemed.

The idea of Voodoo was all-consuming; still, what troubled me most of all was the necromancy spell. Somehow, the young man was lured into the dark ritual. Much like the surrounding everglade, my mind overflowed with questions. Was he forbidden to pass-on for taking part in something so unnatural? Was he cursed to wander between the veils of life and death forever? Why did the girl use the spell in the first place? Did it work? If so, *who* was brought back from the dead?

What happened on that day? *That* was the ultimate question. I had to find the answer and reverse what had been done.

Living deep within my own head, I meandered through the rain, oblivious to the world around me. That was, until a bend in the road, where my racing thoughts screeched to a halt. Frozen in my tracts, I could hardly believe what I was seeing. Blocking the path was a large and fearsome raven.

These birds were everywhere!

My instincts called for me to stay back. Not long before, a raven had tried to attack me from my bedroom window. Plus, there was no forgetting Scarlet Eventide's feathered little friend. Remembering the bird she caged in wrought iron only added to my growing distrust of the animal.

Unnerved, I looked deep into the raven's obsidian eyes. Its intelligent stare was suspiciously familiar. An icy chill rushed through my veins.

It couldn't possibly be the same bird. Could it?

I shook off the ridiculous notion and took a step forward. As I closed in, the raven did not spook or fly away; it gracefully spread its imposing wings. The imperial display was meant to intimidate. Unmoving, we stared each other down—human and animal. My heart skipped a beat and my skin tingled with adrenaline.

Ever so slowly, I reached into my pocket for the rusty knife, but my hand closed around the gris-gris bag instead. Just as I pulled it out, the bird lunged at me, razor-sharp beak open and ready to strike! Caught off guard, I stumbled and fell hard on mucky ground. The impact knocked the wind right out of me. Pain constricted my gut as my mouth gaped, fighting to draw that first painful breath.

The raven took advantage of my vulnerability. Wing feathers splayed, it came down for the kill. The moment its black talons touched my body, the bird was violently thrown off by an unseen force. The beast cowered on the roadside, let out an angry croak, and then took flight to perch in a nearby tree.

I was shocked! The raven wanted to hurt me! It would have succeeded too, if not for . . . whatever that was.

Eyes locked on the raven, I peeled myself off the ground. Thankfully, other than being barefoot and coated in mud, my body was in one piece. Something had protected me!

The gris-gris bag was still in my grasp. I opened my hand to see the little red sack. It looked so unremarkable, resting there in my palm.

Could it be? Did the strange sack of oddities save me?

Again, I looked up at the animal leering overhead. It called out aggressively, neck lunging as it croaked. With the gris-gris bag clutched against my chest, I ran the rest of the way home. Only when Kingsgrove came into sight, did the raven's call fade off to the sound of pouring rain.

✗ ✗ ✗

The weekend had arrived, and with it came sunshine and the *Backwater Summer Fair*. Adalynn and I sat on the steps of Kingsgrove with a pile of wild daisies at our feet. Freshly picked from the roadside, we twisted them into crowns after rescuing my car from down Kings Lane. The walk was very different from the day before.

It amazed me how a little sun could change the entire forest. The gothic world that once was, had transformed. A vibrant spectrum of leafy greens took over the landscape. Even the reaching shadows that nipped at my heels had withdrawn once the sky opened overhead.

As I tossed a daisy stem into the grass, a flock of meadowlarks scattered from a tree in the yard. Seconds later, another car pulled into the grove.

"What a wonderful day," JoJo sang out the driver's side window. She was there for her weekend visit, taking me off the clock and officially granting me my freedom.

Hopping over puddles in the driveway, the nurse made her way to the veranda. "This is for you, Emilie," she said, out of breath, handing me a colorful flyer. It was the summer fair schedule.

"Thanks." I smiled as she joined us on the steps.

Without missing a beat, JoJo was gossiping about people I didn't know and places I'd never been. I listened half-heartedly while glancing over the flyer in my hands. In whimsical script, the *Backwater Summer Fair* was described with zeal. There would be pony rides and petting zoos for the little ones, tents and booths stocked with wares, food, and alcohol for the adults, and games, carnival rides, and sideshows for all to behold. Bands would play up and down the streets, filling Willow Vale with the smooth sound of jazz.

To commence the festivities a dance would be held that very evening. I overheard JoJo going on about who was bringing whom, and the scandals to follow.

Like a spark, an idea came to life in my mind. Before thinking it through, I chimed in, "Why don't you come with me Ada?"

Up until then, I was ready to go by myself. Before arriving at Kingsgrove, being on my own was bearable, comfortable even. The same went for Miss King, yet so much had changed. I had changed. Besides, we were not alone anymore—we had each other.

Without hesitation, Adalynn shook her head no, but I was determined. "Please Ada. Come with me to the dance?"

Wide-eyed, JoJo looked at me, then back at Miss King. "What a lovely idea." She spoke slowly and tenderly to her friend, as if afraid she'd startle her. "Why don't you go, Ada? It'll be good for you, I reckon."

Adalynn's struggle was clear to see. She was a recluse—a shut-in. She found refuge within the walls of Kingsgrove. Those walls kept her hidden from the prying eyes of strangers. They kept her safe.

I reached out and took her soft hand in mine. "Please come with me Ada. I need you to come." It was the truth.

Tears welled in her hazel eyes. She was scared. I squeezed her hand a little bit tighter. The woman breathed a shaky exhale, and my heart leapt in anticipation. When a smile curled at the corner of her lips, I knew the answer. Wiping a stray tear from her cheek, she squeezed my hand back and nodded *yes*.

Amazed, I looked at JoJo in triumph. Her toothy smile gleamed and her eyes glistened. Choked up, the nurse cleared her throat. "Well I'll see you there, Good Lord willin' and the creek don't rise." She flashed me a wink before taking Adalynn by the hand. "Now Ada, you come with me. Let's find you a pretty dress to wear." Arm in arm, the two women went inside. Leaving my daisy crown to wilt in the heat, I followed after.

JoJo's southern drawl resonated from one end of Kingsgrove to the other. Focused on her sweet tone of voice, I walked the hallway to my room. It should have put me at ease, but it did not. The urge to slam the door behind me and hide away still clawed at my insides. I locked myself in then searched every dark corner and patch of light for ghosts. When nothing jumped out at me, I took a few deep breaths to slow my pounding heart. My room smelled like summer, which helped. The midday sun spilled across my bed from the open window. Part of me wanted to bask in the warm light and forget about my troubles. Knowing that was easier said than done, I tore through my wardrobe instead, searching for something to wear at the dance. Shin deep in clothes, I finally slipped into a shift dress made of creamy white lace.

Once my wild hair was tousled and tamed, I glossed my lips then kissed the air in satisfaction. The mirror was being kind at last. My reflection was fresh and freckled, with blue eyes brightened by the sun. Smoothing out the dress, I stepped back to see myself from head-to-toe.

Something was missing. There were no pockets to stash my knife and gris-gris bag.

I dug through my dresser and found a pearl-encrusted purse that once belonged to my grandmother. It was perfect. The look was both effortlessness and polished at the same time. Yes, it *was* perfect—it was the perfect illusion. On the surface, everything looked all right, but on the inside, I was a complete mess. It was foolish of me to ignore what was *truly* missing.

My heart, which was once safely concealed, had unravelled. It happened so quickly—so unexpectedly. A gaping hole was left exposed like a raw wound touched by air for the first time. It stung . . . bad. No wonder I always closed myself off. With my guard down, there was nowhere to hide from the pain. All those who left me forever—all those who mattered most—seemed further away than ever before. Thankfully, Adalynn was by my side. Without that strange and wonderful woman, I had no one and nowhere to belong.

Before losing the nerve, I went to leave and found myself lingering by the bedroom door. The hallways scared me the most. There were too many buried nooks and narrow alcoves where someone could be watching and waiting. Frightened by my own shadow, I practically flew down the many steps to the foyer. I stumbled into a pair of ballet flats and waited anxiously by the front door. Moments later, Adalynn appeared on the landing. For that split second, all ghosts and Voodoo vanished from my mind.

She was captivating.

Vintage yet timeless, Miss King's chiffon dress came just below the knee. Her hair was a mass of silver waves, loosely pinned back with three silk flowers. The mistress of Kingsgrove looked young and happy. From the nervous smile on her face, it seemed she knew it too. I could not imagine the gamut of emotions that clashed inside of her. Without the right words, I just smiled my most encouraging smile and opened the door.

Miss Peters went home to doll herself up, so I drove Adalynn away from Kingsgrove. Over the rumble of the Trans Am, my endless chatter filled the uneasy silence. I was afraid to stop talking. The nervous energy was tangible, and my voice was the only distraction. Considering my own stomach was in knots, Adalynn was surely going through a lot worse. Distracted or not, she just stared out the windshield, tensely clutching her handbag all the way into town.

The fair was in full swing, so I parked outside the downtown core and stepped out of Trans Am. When I opened the passenger door, Adalynn did not budge. Eyes as wide as saucers, she was frozen in her seat, looking out at the crowd. I bit my bottom lip as her expression pierced my heart.

"We could turn around and go home if you want Miss King." I crouched by the open door and rested a hand on her arm. "It's just . . . life is *so* short, you know. Please, don't let it pass you by."

There was really nothing else to say or do to convince her. The fact that she had made it that far was a feat within itself. Fingers crossed, I waited. Then, ever so slowly, her expression changed. There was a spark of strength in her eyes that was not there before. With her back straight and chin lifted, she seemed to banish her once resigned demeanor. All of a sudden, the damaged woman who hid deep in the backwoods of Willow Vale was gone. The elegant and refined Miss King of Kingsgrove had taken her place.

Like a pair of warrior misfits, we took to the street. Adalynn beamed, as an archway of woven branches and lights passed over us. We purchased two tickets, linked arms, and merged with the throng of fairgoers. The scent of kettle-corn and deep-fried funnel cakes filled the air.

My mouth watered. "Are you hungry?" I asked.

Adalynn nodded enthusiastically.

We sat in the grass and shared a dinner of crawfish, biscuits, and snow cones. As the sweet cherry snow melted in my mouth, I began to realize that all eyes were on us. Slack-jawed and shameless, the citizens of Willow Vale were shocked to see the one-and-only Miss King. There were gawkers and pointers from every angle. To my surprise, Adalynn did not seem to notice or appear to care, if she had.

With full stomachs and cherry-stained lips, we left our spot in the grass to wander the lively streets. Colorful banners and ribbons danced in the air as the sun fell to the horizon. I smiled as strings of lanterns came to life against the celestial backdrop. It could not have been a more perfect night.

Following the crowd, we entered a clearing where a makeshift stage and dance floor was laid, hay bales were stacked, and Mason jars glowed with candlelight. Sitting at a nearby table, wearing a pleated denim dress, was JoJo Peters. As we walked over, she stood with both hands clasped over her heart.

Delighted, the nurse called out. "You two are absolutely radiant! Sit. Sit!" She gestured to the table. "Have a mint julep before the dance starts."

The three of us sat, sipping our drinks while the band opened up with a high-spirited tune. Almost instantly, a small clique of socialites approached us.

"JoAnne Peters!" one of the stiff-necked women said in a nasal drawl. "What a pleasure it is to see you." With a fake smile plastered on her face, she looked right at Adalynn. "And who do we have here?"

In her pleasant way, JoJo graciously introduced us. "Good evening, Mrs. Lambert. You know our Miss King, of course! And this here is the lovely Miss Emilie Wyld."

CHRISTENA ROSE

Mrs. Lambert did not even glance my way. Her sights were set on Adalynn. "Miss King? As in, *the* Kingsgrove Estate? Well, bless my stars!"

The socialites knew very well who she was. While they sank their flashy press-on claws into one another, climbing the social ladder, Adalynn was already at the top looking down. Despite her affliction, she was the paradigm of old money and high-society. They could only reach that level of class in their wildest dreams.

"How are you this evenin'?" Mrs. Lambert drawled unpleasantly.

Adalynn nodded politely in response.

Mrs. Lambert chuckled while glimpsing back at her followers. "It's a beautiful night, isn't it?"

Adalynn nodded again.

"I'm so happy to have finally met you. You should really get out more often. In fact, I have a marvellous idea!" Pleased with herself, a Cheshire smile stretched across her face. "Why don't you join us at the next gathering of the WVSC? You'd fit right in."

Mrs. King simply shook her head *no*, then looked away, disenchanted.

"What's a matter Miss. King? Cat got your tongue?" The women snickered, thinking they were so clever.

My jaw dropped in disbelief. No wonder Adalynn stayed locked away in Kingsgrove.

The disgust I felt quickly turned into anger. "Miss King is a very busy woman," I blurted in a spicy tone. "She has prior engagements."

The woman all faced me at once. "Is that so?" Mrs. Lambert replied with arrogance dripping off her painted lips. "Well then . . . I guess we'll be on our way. You ladies have a nice night." They left, towing the tense atmosphere away with them.

Exasperated, I looked at JoJo and asked, "The WVSC?"

"Willow Vale Social Committee," JoJo clarified with a sour look on her face. "Them women are a bunch of uppity crones. It's a good thing you said something, Emilie. I was 'bout to give them a tongue lashing, I swear."

Brows creased, we looked at each other for a moment then burst out laughing. Even Adalynn had a sly smile curled on her face. I was relieved to see her light-hearted mood had not changed. For a moment, I thought the WVSC had ruined everything. Thankfully, Adalynn was unscathed by the tactless bunch. She looked content with her feet tapping to the rhythm of Dixieland.

As the band warmed up, the dance floor began to fill. Children spun hand-in-hand while couples twirled and dipped in each other's arms. Adalynn's eyes sparkled as she watched each person let their inhibitions go as the music played. I put my drink down and stood up to face her.

"Dance with me?" I offered her my hand.

She shook her head in a definitive *no*.

"I won't take *no* for an answer." I winked with a smile. Clutching the skirt of her dress, she looked back at the crowd. "It'll be fine," I kindly assured her.

Cautiously, she took my hand and let me pull her to the floor.

Although tense at first, once the beat livened up, Adalynn loosened up like the others. While I danced lithely and freely around her, the woman's face came to life. My heart swelled at the sight of her tentative but happy moves. After staring death in the face, Adalynn caged herself in a grove of willows as the world grew and changed around her. Hopefully, those days were finally over.

The music slowed and we took our seats. JoJo was in a deep conversation with Mrs. Carmichael from the general store. Adalynn paid them no attention. She just closed her eyes and swayed with the song's smooth melody. My own gaze fell on a young couple holding each other close on the dance floor. The boy ran his hand lovingly through the girl's auburn hair. She rested her cheek to his chest and they moved together as one. They were lost in their own little world of stolen kisses and candy-coated promises.

There was a time when that boy and his girl would have blended in with the background—an out-of-focus-filler on a canvas with a much more interesting subject. While sitting there, mint julep warming in my hand, that boy and his girl were all I could see. I wanted to be her and I wanted him to be the ghost. It was crazy to think it, but I wanted his phantom touch more than any living man's. For days, logic and reason had lost the battle. There was no fight left.

The truth was, I loved him. I was in love with a ghost.

As I finally admitted the sad truth to myself, the pain of loss sharpened. Just before it cut into my already scarred heart, something caught my eye. My heart dashed the readied blade aside and leapt with hope.

Could it be?

My drink nearly slipped through my fingers. I placed the glass on the table, shaking. There was no mistaking that face. It had to be true. Like a dream, he was there, on other side of the teeming dance floor. The young man was there, looking back at me!

In an instant, the world was a blur and everything seemed to move in slow motion. I jumped from my chair and tried to weave through the huddled crowd. It felt like each person that stood between us was there by design, forcing us apart. My head spun as the rhythmic music numbed my senses, consuming me entirely. As if taunting me, the ghost kept moving further away and out of sight. The faster I pushed through, the faster he seemed to fade away.

I broke free of the dance floor just as the young man disappeared behind a nearby tent.

"Hey!" I called into the shadows, desperate and afraid to lose him. He was *so close*.

I hurried to the back of the tent, expecting to see the ghost, but crashed head-on with Ruby Monrose instead.

"Emilie!" she cried out in shock. "What are you doing?"

"Sorry Ruby," I apologised passively, too distracted to even think. Looking over her shoulder, I searched for any sign of the ghost.

"Are you ok, *cherie*?" Her tone was worrisome.

It was too late. The ghost was gone. He vanished into thin air, once again.

My spirit plummeted. "I'm sorry, what?" I blanked, not hearing the question.

She grabbed hold of my shoulders to get my full attention. "I said, are you ok?"

"Everything's fine. I thought I saw someone I knew . . . but I was wrong."

"Are you alone, Miss Wyld?" she asked tenderly.

"No, I came with Miss King." We turned to face the dance floor. "Oh no," I winced. I left Adalynn's side for only a moment; it was just enough time for a snake to slither its way over—a snake named Scarlet Eventide.

HEX ME NOT

"Good evening, Miss Wyld," Scarlet said with her back still facing me, as if she could sense my sudden closeness. My skin crawled at the unsettling thought.

Forcing a smile on my face, I returned the greeting. "Good evening, Miss Eventide."

She twisted her thin frame and flashed me her own perfectly fake smile. "I was just expressing to Miss King what a delight it is to see her." Scarlet's voice was cloying with a sour hint of malice.

I shot a glance at Adalynn. Her face was stripped of its color. Looking dazed and fragile, she reached for JoJo, who took her by the hand and helped the woman to her seat.

My blood boiled.

Scarlet was to blame, without a doubt. I wanted to tell her off right then and there, but my instincts ordered me to stay calm. I bit my tongue and by some miracle, my smile never faltered. Unfortunately, the same went for Miss Eventide. With one look, she unleashed the full wrath of her cool arrogance. Her hard eyes pierced right through me. There was no light in them, just two swirls of grey that emptied into a dark void. Their hypnotic pull just about took my breath away.

The pearls nearly snapped off my purse from the strain of my grip. It took every bit of my strength to keep it together. "I'm sure that's all you were doing." The words hissed through my teeth.

Scarlet cocked her head slightly to one side. She was surprised with my conviction. Her eyes narrowed daringly, and my stomach turned under the heat of her stare. Intimidated or not, the poised mask was in place, and I refused to let it slip. She took a step closer and parted her lips to speak, but was interrupted by the sound of a sweet Creole accent. "*Bonjour* Scarlet."

"Ruby." Scarlet rolled her eyes, clearly unenthused by the librarian's advance.

"I did not know Miss Wyld and you were acquainted." Miss Monrose glanced my way.

"We're neighbors. Isn't that right, Miss Eventide?" I asked fearlessly, knowing very well that I played a dangerous game.

Scarlet's smile was wicked in response. She did not take her eyes off mine as she eluded the question. "Well ladies, this has been lovely, but I must be on my way." The Cimmerian beauty turned gracefully on a black high-heel and slipped into the crowd.

Before I could speak with Ruby, JoJo got my attention. "Miss King seems to have had enough fun for one evenin'. I'm gonna take her home."

"I can take her home! It's no problem," I offered, feeling responsible. Adalynn was leaving because of Scarlet. Instead of chasing ghosts, I should have stayed by her side. If I knew what Scarlet had said to Miss King, it would have explained a lot. What did she want with her anyway? Seeing the effect it all had on Miss King had me more than a little suspicious.

Where did the Eventides fit in? What was going on?

"Nonsense! Stay as long as you like, Emilie. The week is done. You're free to do as you please. Enjoy the festival with Miss Monrose," JoJo insisted, winking at Ruby. "And don't you worry 'bout Miss King. I'll stay with her tonight. She'll be right as rain in the mornin'."

JoJo bid us goodnight and left with Adalynn at her side.

"This is the first time I ever saw Miss King. I've heard of her, of course. Everyone has," Ruby said in wonderment as she watched the two women walk away. "How did you get her to leave that house, Emilie?"

"I asked her to." The answer was simple.

"You have been a blessing to her then," Ruby said earnestly.

The statement rendered me speechless. After seeing Adalynn accosted by Scarlet and the WVSC, it was kind of hard to believe I was a blessing to anyone.

Surveying the crowd, Ruby pulled me in by the lace sleeve and whispered, "Come with me. We have much to speak about."

Ruby and I walked through the grass toward the fair's own amusement park. Night had arrived and the carnival was flashing with lights of every color. Screams of laughter carried through the warm breeze as coaster rides spun and dropped in and out of the sky.

"How do you know Miss Eventide?" Ruby spoke over the mechanical songs that looped perpetually through the park.

Her curiosity did not surprise me. "I wandered into her shop last week."

"You said she was your neighbor? I did not think Miss King had neighbors." Ruby chose her words carefully. She even linked arms with me, preventing my escape. Her questions were nearing a dangerous territory. I had to choose my answers just as carefully. There was no way I could tell her that Kingsgrove was haunted. Being spiritual was one thing, but being attacked by one ghost and falling in love with another was a whole other world of *crazy*.

"It seems that Miss Eventide owns a cabin not far from Kingsgrove. But, I don't think she actually lives there."

"What makes you think that?" Ruby persisted.

"Because, I went there. It was isolated and old, but I couldn't get close enough to know for sure." As the words escaped my lips, I knew it was too much. Ruby seemed to have an effect on me. I wanted to trust her—to trust someone.

"Why couldn't you get close enough?" she asked with her arm still linked tightly with mine.

"The cabin's pretty deep in the forest and it was getting dark. Then I started to feel unwell, so I went home." I tried to sound nonchalant, like it was no big deal.

Ruby's intuition was too sharp. "You felt unwell?"

"Yes."

"Out of nowhere?"

"Yes."

I could almost see the wheels turning in her head.

"When you went to *The Eventide Emporium,* did you leave with anything? Did Scarlet give anything to you?" Ruby's pixie face creased as her tone hardened.

"Oh my God! I completely forgot!" I held the silver locket away from my chest to show Ruby.

"She gave you this necklace?"

"No, not the necklace." Ever so carefully, I opened the locket to display what had been inside the entire time. "This . . ."

It was the tiny dark jewel with a blood red center.

Her golden eyes widened. Holding her breath, she took my hand and gingerly closed the locket with the jewel still inside. She hushed me with a finger then silently beckoned me to follow her. Together we ran through the field, away from the festival. Hand in hand, we weaved through yards and unlit suburban alleyways. The librarian was deft and agile, moving swiftly as she led the way.

While doing my best to keep up, I was itching with concern. Why was Ruby so frantic and freaked out? Where was she taking me?

"Do you have your gris-gris bag with you, Emilie?" Ruby whispered, a little out of breath.

"Yes, in my purse," I said, completely winded and sick with nervous energy.

"Good," she breathed as we ran behind the library. Soon, we were under the willow tree and inside of her little, hidden house. Ruby left me in the entryway to watch her through the beaded curtain. Like a whirlwind, she mindfully filled a canvas bag with a number of items from her chest of drawers. Wasting no time at all, Ruby slung the bag over her shoulder, took me by the arm again, and steered us back outside. I was guided to the middle of her small, fenced-in backyard. Ruby placed the canvas bag on the ground and rooted through its strange contents.

The yard was pitch-black until I heard the strike of a match. Ruby shielded the flickering flame with a hand while lighting the wick of a white and black candle. The orange glow danced in the reflection of her glasses.

"A white and black candle will provide a spiritual blessing and freedom from evil," Ruby explained as she drew a circle of salt around us in the grass.

At that moment, the atmosphere changed. The wind picked up, threatening to blow the candle out. My skin crawled when the harsh croak of a raven followed. We turned and saw the shadowed figure balancing on the wooden fence. Ruby fearlessly walked over to the bird and sprayed it with an arc of salt. The raven lifted with the force of its wings and flew off into the night.

"We must hurry," she said, retrieving a small bottle from the canvas bag. "This is Van Van oil. It will ward off the darkness."

Ruby reached up and pulled my face down to hers. She then proceeded to anoint the top of my head with the oil, tracing it down my forehead over the tip of my nose to my bottom lip. She continued by rubbing the oil over my shoulders, down my arms, torso, and legs. With flourish, she sprinkled the ground around my feet and began to sing.

Ogou Fe Fe Feray o!
Ogou Fe Fe Feray o!
Those who's done good to others, give them life for me
Those who's done bad to others, let their blood runs down
Ogou Fe Fe Feray o!

"What's that song?" I asked nervously once she finished.

"It is a song for Ogou. I do not ask for his favor lightly." She spoke solemnly and handed me a small garden spade. "Now, you must dig." Ruby watched as I knelt on the ground and tore at the dense soil. After the hole was dug, she instructed me to open my locket. "Let the stone fall into the ground and bury it."

With shaking hands, I did as she said, then stood to pack the loose dirt with my feet.

Ruby took the open locket and said, "These are bits of straw from a broom." She then placed the pieces inside, closed the silver pendant, and let it fall back against my chest.

It seemed odd to carry bits of straw around my neck. I had to ask. "What is it for?"

Looking me dead in the eye, she answered. "It will help keep the witches away."

"Witches?" I could not help but laugh.

Ruby's expression was severe, making my face fall in an instant. "Let us go inside where we cannot be heard."

An uneasy feeling sank like a rock to the pit of my stomach. To think someone or something could be listening, lurking, waiting, was pretty frightening. With an unpleasant chill running through my veins, I followed Miss Monrose back into her home.

The door was locked and the candles were lit before we sat cross-legged on the living room floor. I ran my fingers through shag carpet as my mind raced.

What just happened? Was Ruby serious when she mentioned witches?

And here I thought my hands were already full with ghosts and Voodoo.

Ruby's eyes were vacant when she started to speak. "I had a feeling Scarlet had ventured down the left-handed path. But now I'm certain she's lost her way." Staring off into space, she was consumed by the realization. "There was a darkness attached to you. I felt it on the first day we met. After seeing Miss Eventide with you tonight and finding her little gift, I knew where the darkness had come from. I had to cleanse you and free you from its grip. You are protected for now, so we may speak." Just like that, she was back down to earth with her eyes locked on mine.

I took the opportunity to ask, "The jewel . . . what was it for?"

"I do not know for sure. My guess is that the stone was there to form an attachment—to keep a close eye. Scarlet is threatened by you, Miss Wyld." Ruby pushed her glasses up her nose and waited for my response.

"That's not possible." I snickered at the crazy notion. Scarlet's presence was a gale force to be reckoned with. She scared the hell out of me.

"There is no other explanation. She has even sent her *beast* to watch you."

"Beast?"

"The raven," Ruby stated with certainty.

So it was the same bird—the same bird that already tried to attack me . . . twice! My stomach coiled as the truth sunk in. Scarlet had sent her *beast* to do more than simply *watch*.

"You mean to tell me that her raven will do whatever she tells it to?" I gripped the shag, waiting for her answer.

"It is common for a sovereign of the Black Arts to have a beast as a companion. Animals have a powerful spirit, much stronger than we often give them credit. They can be used for sacrifice to have your desires met, or to gain great power. Some even say that these beasts can be used as a vessel for the dead." Ruby saw the bemused look on my face and clarified. "If a witch dies, it is rumored that they can possess an animal to live on."

"So . . ." I paused for a second to unscramble a thought forming in my head. "You're telling me it's possible that, say, Scarlet's mother or grandmother could *be that raven*?" I recalled the moment when Miss Eventide said her bird was *part of the family*.

Could it be true? Did such magic truly exist?

"Yes. That is was I am saying. If her ascendants also practiced the Black Arts then anything could be possible. It is likely that her mother went and taught her. This is something that is often passed down through the generations. The dark power can grow with each progeny."

"Her mother, Dyana, died during childbirth. It was in an old newspaper at the library. I also read that Scarlet inherited the cabin near Kingsgrove from her late grandmother, Olivia." Unfortunately, that was all I really knew about the Eventides. They were a family that protected their checkered past with good reason.

Ruby bit her lips, thinking carefully before she spoke. "Perhaps the grandmother raised Scarlet in this cabin. I have heard of Olivia before. *Manman* once said that she practiced a powerful Voodoo but kept it very private. The locals feared the woman, but would still go to her if they or someone they loved was sick in the hopes of a cure. Her magic was strong, but often came with a price. *Manman* said that smart people would listen to their fears and stay away. Sometimes it is best to die knowing your soul is clean. Papa Legba is more likely to offer his blessing if you meet him on the crossroads with integrity." Ruby stretched out her short legs then asked, "Do you think it was a spell that made you feel unwell near the cabin?"

"Yes, it was a spell. I saw things—things I'll never be able to forget." I shuddered and fought the memory back into hiding.

"I'm not sure why she fears you, Emilie. I know you *also* have your secrets, and maybe one day you will trust me with them. For now, my advice to you is to stay away. It takes much knowledge and clever thinking to overcome these dark powers. Stay away, *cherie*. Stay away."

✗ ✗ ✗

When I returned home that evening, my instructions were clear: I must take a bath to complete the cleansing. However, this was no ordinary bath; it was a ritual with very specific steps that were to be followed with care. I watched Ruby meticulously gather various ingredients and create what she called a tincture: a solution of plant extract including thistles, boneset, hyssop flowers, and cloves. She heated it up on her stove like soup then strained it into a jar. As it steamed and cooled, Ruby combined pounded eggshells and rock salt in a separate container. Once everything was topped off and sealed tight, she bagged the tincture, the container, and three vials labeled as holy water, goat's milk, and Van Van oil. The Van Van oil was not for the cleansing, but for anointing the gris-gris bag and myself for protection.

Standing over the clawfoot tub, I began to add each component to the rising water. My nose wrinkled from the harsh aroma as my shift dress hit the floor. Naked and feeling a bit foolish, I stepped onto a towel and proceeded to scrub my skin pink with a cloth soaked in cold water.

Next, I lowered myself into the bath. The water instantly warmed my body and chased the shivers away. While lying there, I was to speak with the spirit of Ogou. Ruby said that Ogou was commonly known as St. George, who was often described as a soldier fighting a dragon on horseback. Many revered this spirit as a mighty warrior. Apparently, I was in need of one. Even without telling Ruby the whole story, she still believed I was in trouble. The look on her face when she bid me farewell and good luck sent shivers down my spine. Needless to say, if this *warrior* was available, I was not about to turn him away.

As the bath water settled around me, I called to the spirit. "I, Emilie Wyld . . . ah . . . petition Ogou for his favor." The strange words fumbled in my mouth. While thinking of what to say next, the events of those past weeks flashed through my mind. Feeling the full weight of all that lay on my shoulders, my voice quavered. "I know that ghosts are real, and that some are more monster than human. I know this because a man and a woman haunt this house. They are connected in some way, but *how* or *why*, is still a mystery to me. The man says that he's trapped, and the woman . . . she'll stop at nothing to keep me from saving him."

The weight bore down, and a gasp of breath caught in my throat. I pressed my lips together and felt a tear drop from my cheek to mix with the tinted bath. Already lost in the bedlam, I realized there was no point in holding back.

"I ran away from the past and found myself here, in a place that is so far beyond what I expected, and still it feels right. This ghost . . . he changed *everything*. For some reason, we can see each other, and now my life will never be the same. If you deem me unworthy, if you ignore my plea, I will fight for him regardless. It's a promise I intend to keep. But trust me when I say, I need your help. I'm afraid. Afraid of the all the dark things that threaten me, afraid I may join the ghost before I can free him, and afraid to inevitably lose this . . . love . . . that I've only begun to feel."

By asking for the spirit's help, I allowed myself to believe. Having faith in something that you could not see or understand was kind of magical. Like a dream, I could feel myself surrender to the spirit. Back arched and eyes closed, I opened myself up to him. "Please Ogou. Take my hand. Show me the way."

I sat in the tub for some time, letting the water cool before pulling the stopper. As it slowly drained, I visualized the spell from the jewel wash off my body and slip away. With that, the cleansing ritual was complete. Remarkably, the doubt that infested my body for those past few days was gone! The heaviness lifted from my heart, leaving me revived and newly empowered. For the first time in my life, I felt a *real* strength in standing on my own without any walls to protect me. The broken little girl of my past could not haunt me any longer.

There was no way to be sure that Ogou had accepted my petition. There was no way to be sure of anything really, except that Scarlet Eventide was watching. Despite Ruby's warning, I had to find out why. And above all else, I had to find what she was hiding in those woods.

THE VEIL

"Good mornin', Emilie. Don't you look pretty today." The rising sun brightened JoJo's great smile. The first rays of daylight had peeked through the window above the kitchen sink.

A cup of coffee found its way into my hands as I sat at the table gratefully. With a glance around the room, I asked, "Where's Miss King?"

"She's still restin'." JoJo turned away and tried to look busy, wiping the already spotless counter. "Last night was very excitin' for Ada. That kind of exertion can take its toll on someone like her." Her voice faltered, revealing there was more left unsaid.

"Is she ok?" My pitch was high as concern hit me like a dagger to the chest.

JoJo stopped wiping and her shoulders fell.

"Please tell me," I pleaded.

"Miss King has a weak heart." JoJo turned, smile in place. "But there's no need to worry 'bout it, ya understand. She'll be right as rain, soon enough." She gripped my arm for assurance, but her glistening eyes were a dead giveaway.

My heart sank in an instant. I was responsible. Adalynn went to the festival because of me. There was a dull pain blooming in the pit of my stomach—a pain that was all too familiar. When my Nana died, it left a hole in my heart that no one would ever fill. Then, like an unexpected gift, Adalynn came into my life. Without her, I would be alone once again.

The nurse saw my crestfallen face and grabbed a hold of my shoulders. "Don't you go blamin' yourself now, ya hear. Seeing her all dressed up and dancing like that . . . was wonderful. Last night was just the thing she needed. I've never seen her so happy, and I wanna thank you for that." JoJo spoke with sincerity, and I was again lost for words.

After a quiet breakfast with Miss Peters, I found myself sitting in the garden pulling weeds out of a tangled patch of lilies. It was my day off, but I needed somewhere to hide away and think. There were dangerous ideas swimming around in my mind. The peace of the garden was just the place to craft these dangerous ideas into the perfect plan.

I had the upper hand, for a short time, at least. Scarlet's stone was gone, and buried with it was her ability to watch my every move. Eventually, the witch would realize her spell had lifted. I had to get to the Eventides' cabin before that happened.

As the day lingered on, my thoughts reeled with every frightening scenario and outcome imaginable. No matter what path I explored, it came to the same simple truth—there was no time to waste! My only option was to leave at dusk and find the cabin before nightfall. At that hour, the forest would provide the shadows needed to stay hidden. Ruby said it would take knowledge and clever thinking to overcome Scarlet's dark powers. Sneaking into the cabin undetected with the little knowledge imparted by the librarian would have to do. That was the plan, and with any luck, I would leave with some answers.

Eyes narrowed, I ripped the head off a tiger lily and crunched its blood-red petals in my fist. As the flower fell to the ground in pieces, a spark of conviction ignited. Although Scarlet wielded a powerful witchcraft, she had not seen the likes of my wilful determination—a power that would surely take me to the end, wherever the end may be.

✗ ✗ ✗

An orange blaze streaked the sky like a banner saluting the hour of reckoning. I was ready. My messenger bag was strapped on and packed with a book of matches, sea salt, Van Van oil, and the gris-gris bag. The locket of straw was tucked under my hoodie and the rusty knife was stuffed in the pocket of my denim shorts. Lastly, the lantern was topped off with fuel and my sneakers were on with the laces tied tight. My heart pounded with anticipation. These small provisions were my only hope. I feared the ghost would not be there to rescue me, as he had before.

Since the cleansing, it became clear that the ghost at the dance was not my ghost at all. Seeing him was no more than a clever trick to lure me away from Adalynn. Scarlet was trying to seduce us both. Did it mean that the Eventides were connected to the haunting of Kingsgrove? The question continued to wear on my mind. The fact that she was preying on someone like Miss King, was vile, to say the least. She was up to something, and I refused to let her get away with it.

Geared-up and ready to go, I descended the staircase in silence. JoJo and Adalynn were playing cards in the east parlor. Feeling like a fly-by-night vigilante, I hid under my hood, and tiptoed past the open doors. Thanks to the dimly lit hall, the women did not see me sneak into the foyer and out the front door. Fired up with adrenaline, I sprinted across the grounds and passed through the cemetery gate. The willow tree bowed before me in mourning. I stepped lightly under its weeping canopy and crept between the graves up to the river's edge.

Before Kingsgrove was left behind, the stone angels compelled me with their all-knowing eyes. "Wish me luck," I whispered up to them, needing all the help I could get, even if it was from the dead.

The river rushed beneath my feet as I crossed over the old bridge. The hundred-year-old structure moaned and trembled with every footfall. I stalled on the edge where forest began, hesitant to cross that final threshold.

One more step, and there was no going back.

Ruby's warning to *stay away* collided with my own common sense. Then I remembered the young man's face, marred in anguish. The thought crashed through and pushed aside all my sensibilities. I *had* to do this for him, for Adalynn—for me.

Anxiety surged through my veins as I took the first step on that fateful path. Walking the main trail was not an option. When the ghost rescued me in the woods, he said, *They must have seen you coming. Somehow, they can see.* Although the stone was gone, my hackles were up in fear. I kept to the shadows that grew alongside the trail, hoping the plan to go unnoticed may well succeed.

Fallen logs and soggy peat made the journey long and unpleasant. Reaching the cabin before nightfall would be a difficult task. My hand kept wandering to the lantern, which swung precariously from the bag at my hip. No matter how temping, I refused to light the wick until it was impossible to see any other way. At one glance, it appeared that that time would come soon enough. Night leached and prowled as the sun kissed the horizon. The depleting light cast inky shadows that seeped over the forest floor. Cowering in the ferns, I tried to blink away the illusions that took form along the path.

Was that a bewitched raven waiting to attack or just a fallen branch?

Was that a woman with a mane of black hair or just a sapling cloaked in Spanish moss?

Was that a phantom crouching in a tree or just a cypress reaching with a twisted limb?

Fear tapped my shoulder like an unwanted visitor, making its presence known. I was losing control, shooting a cagey look at every distorted patch of darkness. Nerves raked through my body, tensing every muscle until it burned. I was approaching the lion's den with only little charms and blind faith as protection. Without question,

all my common sense had slipped away the moment I stepped foot
in Willow Vale. Even as the fog began to roll in, I chose to ignore
my blaring intuition. Something told me it was more than a harm-
less change in the weather. It happened too quickly. In the blink
of an eye, the crawling mist had devoured the forest in one billow-
ing gulp. Instantly lost and disoriented, my only hope then was to
light the lantern. Kneeling on the damp ground, I unhooked the
handle and found the matches in my bag. Four shaky strikes and
one broken match later, a flame sparked to life and the wick was lit.
To my despair, even the lantern could not penetrate the fog around
me. There was no way of telling which way was up! I spun with the
lantern held high and felt my heart plummet.

What had I done?

Then I heard it . . . *kreeee-arr, kreeee-arr.*

It was not the harsh croak of a raven that I had come to know; it
was the haunting cry of a hawk! Amidst the blackened fog, a realization stunned me like flash of pearlescent light.

The white hawk! Could it be?

There was only one way to know for sure. With my sense of sight
rendered useless, I listened for the distant cry. One step at a time, I
climbed and weaved through the thick undergrowth. The bird called
to me, over and over again . . . *kreeee-arr, kreeee-arr.* I chased after,
trusting the hawk would lead me safely to providence. Then, with
a stumble, I was suddenly free. The air cleared so abruptly that I
turned and staggered back out of shock. The dense wall of vapor was
behind me. From that side, the barrier looked so bizarre and unnatural. It writhed with coiled fingers of mist, flicking and clawing at the
air to pull me back in. Stepping further away, I turned and finally
saw it—the Eventide's cabin.

The world I had breathlessly stumbled into seemed to pulse
before my eyes. It was a sinister-looking place, caged in a ring of
petrified oaks. The small log structure appeared to have been aban-
doned many years before. It had a roof that sagged and a foundation

that was being swallowed by the ground beneath it. A dilapidated porch coated in moss and rot was barely hanging on by its rusted nails. The soft wood buckled under my weight as I climbed the steps. There was no breeze, yet a chorale of chimes rang above me. The entryway was decorated with many bizarre trinkets and charms. I ducked to avoid them, afraid to stir the trickery that hung, waiting.

Once on the porch, my heart leapt in surprise. The lantern cast its light onto the large skull of an alligator. It hung next to the front door, as if guarding the cabin's entrance. The beast's gnarled grin was unwelcoming, to say the least.

Message received.

Just below the skull was a heap of old animal traps and snares. Still locked inside of one was the skeleton of a bird. It was all that remained of a life cut short—a life imprisoned and forgotten. The sight of the little creature tore my heart into pieces. It was just lying there all broken and alone.

Feeling a strange affinity for the bird, I knelt before the trap and pried at the rusty hatch. The wire cut painfully into my hand, but, with determination, it eventually broke and creaked open. "You're free now," I whispered. It was hard to witness such a sad fate, even in that awful place.

I bit a quiver from my lip and stood to face the cabin door. It stared back, pulsing, daring me to go in. Swallowing the lump in my throat, I snuck over to the front window. The smoky glass, being thick with filth, only reflected the light of my lantern. It was impossible to see in. Still, the house felt bleak and empty. No one lived there. The forsaken cabin was shrouded in darkness, inside and out.

Convinced I was alone, I grabbed the handle on the front door. It was locked tight, as expected. Embracing my inner-vigilante, I took a deep breath and hip-checked the old door. Pain was the only result. All the nerves in my body shook with the blow. After taking a moment to regain composure and psych myself up, I slammed my body against the door a second time. My side stung, and yet, despite the pain, a smile spread across my face. The decrepit wood was starting to crack and split! Thrilled, I took a running start and threw all my weight into the final strike. The door busted at the lock and swung open into the house. Its hinges let out a wailing screech and the cabin emitted an unearthly shudder. The tremble was a foreboding enigma—a warning to the unwelcome.

I tried my best to ignore the fear that instantly consumed me. My legs shook as I walked into the dark cabin. My lantern illuminated the space, and the feeling of déjà vu instantly came over me. I had been there before. Not there physically, but in a dream. I could almost hear the Latin chant emanate from the four walls around me. I could imagine myself still in the rafters, silently looking down. I could still see where the young man sat as the girl circled him like a bloodthirsty panther—the same girl who haunted Kingsgrove as a young woman.

What did it all mean?

Was this her home? Was she an Eventide?

The riddle began to untangle, only to raise more questions as the pieces started to fit.

Was she the one? She had to be.

I knew that it had to be true. The woman who haunted Kingsgrove was Dyana Eventide.

That would explain the nightgown soaked in blood. Her life was lost while giving birth to Scarlet over thirty years before. She was wearing it at the moment of her passing. Both Dyana and the young man appeared as they were when death came for them. It had to be true. I felt foolish for not making the connection before. There was even a striking resemblance to Scarlet that I had overlooked. There were too many distractions to notice they shared the same complexion and black hair. I was too overwhelmed to realise they had a similar face and figure. And, I was too petrified to see they had the very same cruel, empty, grey eyes. So that was it. It finally made sense why Scarlet was watching me. Her mother Dyana was trying to stop me. Together, they fought to keep me from releasing the young man from the spell once cast.

I still had no idea who the man was, or what was prevented his spirit from moving on. Also, why was Dyana using necromancy in the first place? Whom was she trying to bring back to life? In the dream it looked like she was stealing life away, not giving it back. I was still so confused, but one thing was crystal clear. I was standing in the Eventide's cabin. If I didn't uncover the truth soon and get out fast, either Scarlet or Dyana would come and find me.

I placed my lantern on a small dinner table that stood in the middle of the cabin. With the wick raised, it was just bright enough to see throughout the space. The small home consisted of one simple room that had been terribly neglected. It smelled of damp mildew and rotten lumber. Kingsgrove had certainly seen better days, but it was nowhere near that far-gone. For a small moment, my heart actually went out to Scarlet. She was a young girl who grew up with very little. No one deserved that kind of poverty, even someone who was instilled with such darkness. No wonder Dyana chose to haunt the estate instead of the cabin in the woods. An eternity spent in that horrible place would be like existing in misery itself forever.

It all made me wonder how the Eventide's felt about living in the shadow of Kingsgrove. Having all that lavish wealth towering over them would have been a bitter pill to swallow. I had my doubts that the Kings and Eventides ran in the same social circles. I could not imagine Olivia and Evelyn chatting over a cup of tea, or Dyana and the twins playing in garden. The King family owned the mill and was very well respected. The Eventide family practiced a dark craft with an income provided only by the desperate and ill. They were witches. Their kinds just did not mix.

I had no clue what it was I was looking for once inside the cabin. There was a very small kitchen in one corner. It had a wood stove, an enamel sink and hand-operated water pump. The back wall was covered with wooden shelving. It was stocked with many unmarked bottles and vials. I gagged at the sight of two large jars in particular. They were brimming with a dark yellow liquid and floating within was a pickled rattlesnake and the bloated carcass of a bullfrog.

On the other side of the room was a single bed with a low table pushed against the footboard. It was where a Voodoo alter had been created. It was very much unlike the one on Ruby's mantel. The tribute to Saint Philomena was a vibrant offering to receive good fortune, strength, and love. The Eventides shrine was quite the opposite.

I knelt in front of the table and tried to make sense of its contents. In the middle, wearing a ratty top hat was a human skull. I had no doubt that it was real. Clenched between what teeth it had left, was a half-burned cigar. Sitting before the skull was a wooden bowl. There was a small dagger resting inside. There was a dried, rust-colored splatter on the blade and at the bottom of the bowl.

Is that blood?

The thought made my skin crawl. Ruby had said, *With sacrifice you can gain great power.* The dark shrine left me wondering how powerful Scarlet actually was. It was apparent that I was in over my head.

Many other gifts were placed ceremoniously before the skull. There was a deck of cards, black and red candles, stacks of coin, a fertility idol, jewellery, locks of black hair, a mummified bat, and a bottle of whisky, all intricately connected by the weave of a spider's web. Whatever favor the Eventides were after, it could not have been good.

The disturbing setting left me thoroughly terrified. I was inside the witch's lair and clearly at the disadvantage. My virtue was no match for that kind of evil. Desperately in need of leverage, my eager search continued. I looked under the bed, inside every drawer, behind all the furniture and in every crate and coffer. There were not many hiding places throughout the tiny cabin. I was bewildered and utterly frustrated. There had to be something. There had to be a piece of the puzzle that I was missing.

I stood in the center of the room and looked around one last time. Out of disappointment, I ran hands over my face, rubbed the back of my neck, and looked up. In that moment something peculiar caught my eye. Hanging on, like my last bit of hope, was a small pouch tied to a rafter. My heart leapt. Why would a witch tie a pouch that high up and out of sight? What secrets were sealed within? Perhaps there was nothing of significance hiding in the deep shadows overhead. Nevertheless, there was only one way to find out for sure.

Without wasting any more time, I dragged the dinner table over and climbed on. I stood on my tippy toes and tried desperately to reach up. The pouch still dangled just out of reach and hung from an awkward angle. I had to get higher. There were a couple wooden chairs scattered around the cabin. After getting down, I took one over and lifted it onto the table. The makeshift structure wobbled as I climbed back up and stood on the seat of the chair. At that point, the only option was to get onto a cross beam and carefully maneuver my way toward the pouch. So, I swung a leg over and positioned my body on top of the closest beam. My face rested against the timber and my arms and legs were wrapped firmly around. I hooked my ankles together and took a few steady breaths. Dust tickled my nose and caught in the back of my throat. I coughed in reflex and watched the grey filth fall gracefully to the cabin floor.

Eventually, I felt secure enough to sit up. My thighs burned from grasping tightly to the beam. Using my hands, I pulled and shifted my body slowly over to the pouch. Finally, I could reach the rope it was tied with. It must have been there forever, since the knot was fused with age. Time passed painfully as I struggled to loosen it. My fingers were raw and my nails broke, but I refused to give in. At last, the knot gave and the sack was free. The anticipation was killing me. Before getting back down to solid ground, I steadied myself and opened it.

Ever so slowly, I reached in and pulled out a small Voodoo doll. I had never seen anything like it. Someone had taken their time to fashion the creepy little poppet. It was definitely meant to be female. The body was stuffed and wrapped in cotton. It had brown human hair on its head and delicate floral fabric sewn to the torso. The mouth of the poppet was gagged with a strip of red cloth and the hands were cuffed together with the same material. It was exactly what I had been looking for. Ruby said these dolls were hidden to prevent discovery and if a poppet is found the magic can be removed or avenged. The poppet was right there in my hand. I could take it with me and finally leave the cabin for good. Once back at Kingsgrove, I would be able to protect myself. It would give me the chance to figure out whom the doll was connected to and how to break its spell.

I opened my leather satchel and stuffed the poppet inside. There had to be a way to remove whatever hex or curse it had created. After who knows how many years, the tormented soul was finally in good hands. With that, I fastened the buckle on the bag and tightened the strap around me.

Just before climbing down, I glanced back at the flannel sack and realised it was not empty. In haste, I reached inside again. As my fingertips touched an item, a shock of electricity nearly knocked me off of the rafter. The muscles in my body convulsed with each wave of pulsing energy. It took every bit of my strength just to hang on. The sensation embraced me, consumed me, and devoured me all at once. Only *one* spirit could make me feel the way I felt at that moment. The young man was there. He was trying to get through to me, and as I pulled out a second doll, I knew why. It was his! It was his poppet.

The doll was completely bound from top to bottom in a veil of black lace. Its face was concealed and the arms and legs were restricted by the many layers. I could not take my eyes off of it. My vision tunneled and only the poppet seemed to exist. Behind all that lace and cotton was the essence of a human life. Resting in my hand was a life that had been controlled and manipulated for too many years. The weight of that realization came crashing down on my shoulders. I had to find a way to save him. It was time to set him free.

While trying to stuff the young man's poppet in my bag, I saw my own breath appear like a puff of frosty smoke. The air around me had turned frigid and icy chills crept their way up my bare legs. It was a warm summer night. There was no explanation for that sudden drop in temperature.

Then I heard . . . *drip* . . . *drip* . . . *drip* . . . *drip.*

FROST AND FURY

Dyana!

Instinct took over and I stashed the poppet in the front pocket of my sweatshirt. There was no time to hide it safely in my bag with the other doll. My eyes shot down and searched every corner of the dismal cabin. There was no sight of the phantom. Still, I could hear the sound, *drip . . . drip . . . drip . . . drip*. It followed the pounding rhythm of my beating heart.

The only place left to look was up. With dread, I slowly peered to the ceiling above. Crouched in the highest peak like a leering arachnid, was Dyana. I screamed in horror as she sprung down on top of me. The impact felt like an arctic blast of pure power. Together, we fell to the table below and smashed it to pieces. I fought to lift my aching body out of the splintered wood. Before I had a chance to escape, Dyana picked me up and threw me effortlessly across the room. My body collided brutally with the shelving on the wall. Glass bottles came crashing down and spilled their vile contents on the cabin floor. A flash of pain assaulted me, and bright stars blinded my vision. I scrambled to rise up and regain some control before Dyana could attack again.

The phantom was blocking the cabin door—the only escape. We stood there staring wildly at one another. The moment was full of a raging intensity. She had a fierce and beautiful face that was contorted by sheer hatred. Her translucent body wavered and flickered in and out of sight.

Why was she filled with such revulsion? Why was she so determined to keep the young man trapped?

"You can't keep him, Dyana," I told the ghost. Her feral expression softened ever so slightly. It was only for a second.

Dyana tilted her head to one side like a twitchy bird. Then her lips curled into a small smile that slowly turned into a grin. It was not a friendly expression. It was scornful and followed by laughter that overflowed with pure malice. It was a chilling promise that echoed all around me. A reverberation of hisses and ghastly taunts surrounded me. The malevolence was so tangible; it even left a metallic taste on my tongue. Dyana's laughter turned gradually into a high-pitch scream as she charged straight at me.

This time I was ready.

I tucked and rolled away from her attack. My quick thinking took Dyana by surprise, giving me the chance to escape. I took a run for it, but she was too quick. While my back was turned, the ghost struck me from behind. The blow sent us both flying through the doorway of the cabin. We tumbled onto the porch and down the front steps. Feeling her phantom flesh against mine was like touching frozen steel. It burned and scorched my skin as we wrestled.

Dyana was ravenous with a thirst for blood. I knew I could not kill her. She was already dead. I had to outsmart her. I had to use the weapons given to me. I channelled all my strength and passion into one kick to her back. The ghost went flying. Her body passed right through the trunk of a nearby tree.

There was just enough time to reach into my messenger bag. My hand closed around the vial of Van Van oil. A split second later, Dyana was on me again. She wrapped her icy fingers firmly around my neck. The oxygen in my lungs escaped instantly. I could feel her hands pass through my skin and grip painfully onto my windpipe. My eyes bulged and my chest tightened as my body fought futilely for air. Just before the world turned dark, I lifted my arm and crushed the glass vial in my fist above her head. The oil seeped between my fingers onto her black hair, down her face into her eyes. Dyana released me and staggered back. I dropped to the ground on my hands and knees and drew a deep quenching breath. While gasping desperately for relief, I watched as the ghost clawed at her face. She shook violently back and forth and wailed hauntingly.

"You can't keep him, Dyana." My voice was strained and breathless. "You can't keep him." As my last words hung heavily between us, the young woman disappeared. I stood on weak legs and brushed the dirt off my sweatshirt.

Was that it? Did I win? Just as my hopes began to lift, I heard a cloying voice from somewhere behind me. "Hello, Miss Wyld."

I spun around and saw Scarlet Eventide emerge from the surrounding fog. She wore tight black pants, knee high boots, and a crop top the color of wine. Her black hair was sleek and her cream-colored skin was radiant. The Cimmerian beauty was stunning and fierce. Next to her, I looked like a fair and delicate child.

I stepped back as she approached. "I see you have met my mother. She does not like you very much." She continued her steady advance on me. "You've been a foolish, young woman, meddling in things you cannot begin to understand." As she spoke, I managed to pull out the canister of sea salt from my bag. I opened the spout and shook the white granules onto the ground around me. Scarlet stopped and giggled. "Clever girl." She placed and hand on her hip. "Perhaps there is more to you than meets the eye. But, I doubt it."

"What makes you think you know anything about me?" I said angrily.

"You ran away from a pathetic past only to fall into the arms of a dead man." The witch threw her head back and let out a venomous laugh. "A man you can never have. He belongs to my mother."

"He belongs to no one!" I snapped. "She trapped him. He wants to be free!"

Scarlet circled me slowly with her arms folded across her chest. Her eyes seemed to search my protective barrier for any weakness. I stood in the center and felt vulnerable at the sight of Scarlet's confident smile. The witch stopped, looked me directly in the eyes and declared. "My mother . . . gave the soldier . . . what he asked for."

Soldier? I imagined during that time, most young men were. WWII ended in the 1940s. He seemed to be from that time. It made sense.

I glared at Scarlet and argued. "Your mother caused only suffering. The only thing she gave him was a curse!"

"My mother gave him exactly what he wanted!" Scarlet yelled. Her anger was so fervent the ground rumbled in response. "My mother gave *everyone* what they wanted, including my grandmother! Then you come along. You came here and tried to take away the only thing *she* wanted. This will never happen, Miss Wyld. I won't let it."

"I'm not trying to take anything. Your mother is the one who did the taking. She stole his life, for what?" My heart pounded while I attempted to hide the fear in my voice.

"Foolish girl. You know so little. My mother only saw an opportunity. She could not have him in life, so when the deal was struck, it gave her a chance to have him in death." I wanted to hit the smug look off of Scarlet's face as she spoke.

"You're talking about murder!" My tone was that of disgust. What deal would have been worth the price of death? I felt dizzy as the witch filled my mind with more riddles. She said Dyana had given her mother something as well. I was so confused. She thought it was important enough to mention. Was it all connected?

Scarlet must have read my mind as she went on. "My grandmother made my mother promise to continue the Eventide bloodline. So that's what she did. She gave *me* to her. Once she fulfilled that promise, she left me behind and joined the soldier. My mother suffered the ultimate sacrifice to be with that man." Scarlet's eyes were full of rage.

"She didn't give you up. She died giving birth to you. It wasn't a choice," I said.

"Your naivety humors me, Miss Wyld. As soon as I was born . . . as soon as I took my first breath of life, my mother killed herself." Scarlet's grey eyes narrowed while she spoke. She did not seem bothered that her mother chose to be with the young man instead of her.

"Why would she do that to you . . . to herself?" I was appalled. Dyana was insane to go to such extremes.

"For love, my dear Miss Wyld. So yes, he belongs to her. He will always belong to her." Scarlet's voice matched her sinister smile.

The envy I felt was like poison invading my heart. Doubt consumed me and had me question all that I had come to believe. Did the young man love Dyana? Was she right to hate me?

As soon as my guard was down, the raven appeared. Its talons were spread and its jet-black wings flapped viscously in my face. It did not breech the sea salt but the sudden onslaught was enough to spook me. With crossed arms, I guarded my face and fell to the ground outside the circle. Before I had a chance to recover, an unseen force lifted my body and pinned me hard against a nearby tree. Scarlet held me from a distance with an outstretched arm. The pressure on my body was painful and unsettling. I could feel the dark energy prick my skin like a thousand tiny needles. I was powerless, paralyzed, and could hardly open my mouth to speak.

Scarlet laughed hysterically at her success. "I knew you would be easy to dispose of, Miss Wyld. Without the man's help, you are pathetic." Debris from the forest floor spun around her as she manipulated the elements. "It was so easy to weaken him. I just pushed him a little deeper into the dark. He was getting a little too close to you. It will take quite some time before he can fight his way back and regain strength. It won't matter anyways. You will be gone soon enough. With a pretty soul as pure as yours, the crossover will be simple! You will never see the soldier again."

I was as good as dead. Scarlet was about to end my life with no remorse. "How?" I managed to whisper through my frozen lips. All the preparations, the cleansing ritual, the gris-gris bag, the spells, were all useless against her.

Scarlet approached with her arm still extended. The raven glided in the sky above. With her free hand, she hooked a finger around the chain holding my locket. "You mean this? You think a little straw is going to help you? I have more power then you and your little friend Ruby can even begin to imagine." The witch yanked and broke the thin, silver chain. She then heartlessly tossed my grandmother's locket into the dirt. "These little charms and superstitions have very little effect on me. My strength is unrivalled, Miss Wyld. All thanks to my grandmother." At that remark, the raven swooped down and perched on Scarlet's outstretched arm. The witch stroked the bird's feathers in reverence. With a curled finger, Scarlet tilted the raven's beak up to face her and nuzzled it tenderly. I knew then that the raven was possessed by Olivia's spirit. When her old body had become useless, she overcame another's. Such a thing could go on for an eternity. It was a scary thought to think the Eventides could live forever, in such a way.

"The time has come, my dear. Together, we will end this." With a small gesture of the hand, Scarlet pulled me away from the tree. She pointed to the ground and my body hit the earth with force. I was a marionette, and Scarlet had the strings.

The witch proceeded to drag my defenceless body ruthlessly through the forest. It was an awful sensation to have absolutely no control over my own body. There was nothing more violating and demeaning than to be treated in such a horrific way.

My flesh burned raw as she pulled me over every rock and root. There was no way to suppress my cries of pain. Scarlet stopped suddenly. I could hear her breathe out a long sigh of irritation. She came over to me and knelt on the ground. With the palms of her hands, she held my face. The witch's vapid eyes peered into mine.

She smiled sweetly, closed the space between us, and kissed me softly on the lips. At first, I was confused by the strange and conflicted endearment. However, when the witch pulled away, I understood completely. Scarlet had stolen my voice. When she continued to pull me helplessly along, I was forced to suffer in silence.

My eyes filled with tears as the waning moon taunted me with its crooked smile. I failed Ada, I failed the young man, and I failed myself. Scarlet *was* too powerful. It was foolish to think someone like me could defeat the witches of Willow Vale. Nothing worked out the way I had hoped. I was supposed to paint pretty pictures and happily lose myself in the charm of Kingsgrove. Instead, I lost myself in the arms of a ghost and was about to die as a result. This was not the way my life was meant to end.

Eventually, Scarlet dragged me onto the bridge. I saw the silhouettes of stone angles through the trees and heard the rushing current beneath me.

"I have been waiting to do this since the first moment I laid eyes on you. You see, Miss Wyld, *this* was all meant to be. Once I throw you in the river, you will drown. It is so deliciously symbolic that I can hardly contain myself." Scarlet's laughter was an expression of sheer satisfaction. I was at the mercy of a psychopath.

The witch raised her hand to cast the final command. Just as my life flashed before my eyes, a tiny voice rang through the darkness. "Let Emilie go!"

Scarlet spun around. Standing on the edge of the cemetery were Ruby Monrose and Adalynn King. A mixture of hope and concern tugged unbearably at my heart. These were two people I cared for. Ruby was my friend and Ada . . . well Ada had become much more than that. If something bad happened to either one of them, it would be my fault. My actions had brought Scarlet there. The witch was evil. She would not hesitate to kill us all if it meant helping Dyana.

"Go home, Miss Monrose. This does not concern a sad little root-worker like yourself. But you," Scarlet pointed to Miss King, ". . . you can watch. Bringing pain to the King family gives me great joy."

The witch scrutinized Adalynn for a moment and smiled wickedly. "Well well. From what I see here, the end is near for you. And what a shame it is that the Kings weren't able to make some dear little ones." Feigning compassion, Scarlet theatrically wiped a non-existent tear from her cheek. "Kingsgrove will sell very soon and it *will* become mine. You'll never be able to drive my mother away again. It will be her home, where she can stay with him forever."

Had the Eventide witches done something to the King sisters in the past? I wondered. Like some sort of infertility spell to prevent them from having children? If that was the case, they could just sit back and wait. Eventually, all the Kings would die. Time would do the dirty work for them. Without lifting a single finger, an entire family would be eradicated. Adalynn was the last King alive. Once she was gone, Scarlet could legally purchase the estate. The witch was born into poverty, but she did not live in the woods any longer. Perhaps she was prepared to buy Kingsgrove when the time came. Perhaps that had been the Eventide's plan all along.

If Scarlet planned to take Kingsgrove for herself, how could I stop her? I was in the middle of a nightmare and there was no waking up.

"Goodbye, our little alabaster princess." The witch had her attention back on me. She took me by the arms and lifted my limp body up against the bridge railing. I could tell by the look on her face that the time had come. Her dark power had risen up around us. She conjured a windstorm that spun our hair together in a cyclone of white and black. Her eyes locked with mine. She had me instantly hypnotized with the whirling abyss of her hollow gaze. The trance scrambled my mind into a dizzy mess.

The witch had manipulated my deepest convictions. I thought, *It would be easy to just give up. I'm so tired—so tired of fighting. All I have to do is surrender and my troubles will be over. Scarlet is here to grant me my liberation.* I smiled blissfully at the enemy. I truly believed that she was my savior.

Then everything changed with a single strike of a match.

Ruby's face was illuminated by the dark blue candle in her hands. With her pretty Creole voice, she sang.

Ogou Fe Fe Feray o!
Ogou Fe Fe Feray o!
Those who's done good to others, give them life for me
Those who's done bad to others, let their blood runs down
Ogou Fe Fe Feray o!

The faint smell of tobacco mixed with the turbulent air. It was followed by the thundering gallop of a horse. The rumble seemed to resonate from everywhere and all around us.

"No," Scarlet whispered and released her hold on me. I fell on the bridge, and the witch looked nervously toward the forest. "Not Ogou. It can't be. He comes for no one." The fierce and beautiful witch was actually frightened.

My eyes watered as the atmosphere hummed and sparked with power and anticipation. The thunderous gallops were closing in. The sound reached a deafening volume and then . . . time stopped. The fervent wind became calm and still, with leaves and dirt frozen in midair. It felt like a dream as a warrior approached me. He appeared as a brilliant mass of pure, white energy. With an unseen force, he untied the spell that bound me.

I was set free.

My mind cleared and my body belonged to me once again.

The warrior reached out and offered me his hand. I lifted my arm and took it gratefully. His touch soothed and invigorated my spirit as he helped me to my feet. For whatever reason—whatever strange reason—the warrior had chosen me. He deemed me worthy of his favor.

As quickly as Ogou came, he was gone again. His gift to me was simple—a fair fight. So, when the world around me came to life and time started once more, I was ready.

Scarlet was visibly shocked to see me standing of my own free will where I had laid a moment before. Her spell had broken. Before she could react, I punched her right square in the face. The witch shrieked, flew back, and fell hard on the wooden bridge. Her spine curled and she clutched her face in pain. I shook off my aching hand and looked toward the cemetery.

My heart shattered.

Ruby was kneeling over Miss King. The woman's body was crumpled in the grass, lying motionless beneath the willow tree.

"Ada!" I cried and Ruby looked up.

"Emilie! Watch out!" she shouted, but it was too late. Scarlet was already on top of me. Beautiful face warped in rage, the witch snarled like a rabid wildcat and pushed me off the bridge.

The ground was stolen from under my feet. The world tilted and flipped around. Down I went with a great crash, breaking through the choppy surface. My body vanished. The river, eager and merciless, took me as its own.

WHITE HAWK

It was not long before the eager river dragged me below its surface. My only source of precious, life-giving air was stolen away. I opened my eyes and saw only darkness. The undertow was strong and the water was deep. My muscles burned as I fought the current. There was no escape. I pushed and pushed through the torrent, only to fall deeper into the watery grave.

At first, the fight to survive was visceral. My adrenalin fueled the battle until exhaustion overwhelmed me. No matter how hard I tried, the water tossed me to and fro, like a leaf in the wind. While fighting the instinct to part my lips and take a breath, my fate became very clear.

I was going to die.

An odd feeling of purpose came with the realization. Before the river claimed me, I *had* to make a choice. With the final moments of my life, I chose to save another.

I pulled the knife out of my shorts, and pried open the rusty blade. As fate would have it, the soldier's poppet was still tucked inside of my sweater. I took it out and immediately went to work while tumbling with the current. With a desperate grip and a bit of trouble, I wedged the blade under a piece of the old lace. The corroded steel was just sharp enough to cut through the twisted veil. I let the knife go and felt for the loose strip of fabric. With the frayed end in my hand, I used my last bit of strength to unravel the poppet.

As the black lace was swept away, a vision flashed in my mind. I could see the young man stepping out of the darkness into the light. The soldier ran through an open field and the brilliant sun shone just for him. His curse was broken. The ghost was free.

Now that my quest was complete, I could surrender my mortality. It would not take very long. Every bubble that floated upward carried away a tiny piece of my life.

There was no air left.

I was drowning.

I could feel myself dying as the poppet left my weary hand. A final tear escaped me, and was lost to the callous river. The fight was over, and I lay to rest in the underwater tomb.

When death came for me, my sorrow was taken away in a single moment. Something truly amazing appeared. The dark water was suddenly ablaze with the most radiant light. I could see the luminous wings of a descending bird. It was a white hawk. I was so awestruck by the animal's strength and beauty that my fear was forgotten. It was there for me. It was there to lift my soul from the deep.

Would it bring me to meet my mother? Would my nana be there?

Would it bring me to the same open field where the soldier ran? Perhaps the sun would shine for us both.

As the hawk went to embrace me with its marvellous wings, something came crashing through the water. It smashed right through the celestial bird and destroyed it. *No!* I screamed in my fleeting mind. The white feathers scattered gloriously through the water, then everything went black.

✗ ✗ ✗

I could feel my soul being lifted up and carried into a dream. It was like a dream I had had once before . . .

> *Two strong arms cradled my wet, limp body. My clothes were twisted so tightly around me, it was*

strangulating. I tried to open my eyes to see who held me so close. My eyelids were so heavy—so very heavy and weak. Then I heard a young man. He was gasping for breath between each heart-wrenching cry. At one point, he lost his footing and we fell to the earth. The young man dissolved into tears as he attempted to gather me in his lap. I wanted, so badly, to reach up and comfort him. I wanted to tell him that everything was okay, but I could not move. I was so weak. He rocked me in his arms and wailed. "No . . . Emilie! You can't die. You can't!" It was too late. I drowned in the river.

I was dead.

I was dead, so why was I dreaming? Why was I not at the crossroads awaiting judgement? Was I unable to move on? Was my soul trapped in a perpetual nightmare?

Had I become the ghost?

It was too much to bear. I was supposed to be with my mother and my nana. I was supposed to be with the soldier. I cried out in anguish, "No!"

"Emilie! You're alive!" The stranger in the dream rejoiced despite the truth. I was dead. I had drowned. "You're breathing!" He mocked me still. "You did it, Emilie! My beautiful, remarkable girl."

Remarkable girl?

The soldier called me that once.

"Please, Emilie. Open your eyes."

My lip quivered—my eyelids fluttered—my heart pounded.

My heart?

In an instant, my eyes were wide open; they looked directly into another's, which were stunning shade of hazel. "I'm sorry," I whispered.

"Why are you sorry? You did it, Emilie. I'm free." The young man was holding my lifeless body in the dirt. If he was in the dream, then I had failed. He was still a ghost.

"I died. I'm a ghost, just like you." My tears flowed with regret. "I failed."

"Oh Emilie, don't cry. That's not true." His smile gleamed. "You're alive . . . just like me!"

In disbelief, I ran my shivering hands over my face then down my wet body. It felt real. I reached up and touched the soldier's cheek. There was no electrical charge. There was no static spark. His skin was soft and warm.

"How?" I was so confused.

Was I?

Was he?

"I was trapped in the dark." The soldier's voice was grave as he explained. "It was like a chamber of nothingness. A pitch-black, hollow place, stuck somewhere between life and death. It's where all restless souls are, just waiting to be forgotten. She's a witch, Emilie. She has powers . . . like magic. Magic trapped me where I could never be at peace. But *magic* can always be undone." The soldier brushed the damp hair off my face. "Don't you see, Emilie? I was never dead."

"You weren't?" My brows creased and my voice was small and uncertain.

He chuckled softly. "No."

"So you're alive?" I asked again.

He nodded yes.

"And, I'm alive?"

He nodded yes and smiled tenderly.

So it was not a dream. He was free! The entire time, I thought his freedom came with a price. He did not crossover, because he was never dead in the first place.

I was shocked and utterly speechless. There were no words. *Words* could not express the thrills that consumed me.

Without wasting another second, I reached up and pulled him in. He accepted me completely. Our lips met. His touch was undeniably organic. It surrounded me like a waterfall of the pure warmth. It was raw, it was natural, and it was real.

We were victorious! He was alive, I was alive, and we were together.

Our chests heaved with want. We fought for air as we drowned in each other's embrace. The soldier pulled away and made a path down my neck with his soft lips. A blitz of pleasant chills trailed across my skin. I arched my back and sighed with ecstasy.

As our bodies tangled together in the weeds, he whispered breathlessly in my ear, "I love you, Emilie Wyld."

"I love you too," I replied with absolute certainty.

He pulled away, and our eyes met. He ran his fingers through my damp hair, and I looked up at him in awe. It was an absolute miracle. A mysterious soldier, who was frozen in time a half a century ago, had not aged a single day. He was given his life back—a life with me in it.

I smiled up at him and asked completely awestruck, "How is this all possible?"

"You saved me. I don't know how, but you did. When that witch pushed you in the river . . ." His voice caught in his throat. He took a deep breath to calm himself before going on. "I was scared. I wasn't strong enough to save you. My biggest fear was about to come true. It was about to happen again. Someone I love was going to die,

CHRISTENA ROSE

because of me. It was all my fault." He buried his face in his hands
in shame.

The young man was shaking as he recalled a painful memory.
"She died because of me, Emilie. If I hadn't left her . . . oh Emilie,
if I hadn't left her in that tree to save the hawk, she never would
have fallen."

The soldier's story was full of regret. It hurt to see him that way.
To ease his pain, I sat up and held him in my arms. He leaned into
my embrace, and went on. "I had never seen such a beautiful bird. I
had just come back from the war, where everything was so ugly." He
shuddered. "When I saw the bird in the trap, it made me so angry.
They were going to take something beautiful and kill it! There was no
way I could let it happen!" The soldier looked up to the blackened
sky. His eyes glistened in the moonlight. "You see, I left home for a
long time and she wanted to know why. She wanted to know what it
was like to fly a plane, just like me. So, I showed her the world from
high above. We climbed the tree and stayed there awhile, looking
down at the river. I told her stories about where I'd been—about
what I'd saw. I left out the bad parts. It wasn't hard. Those were the
things I hid deep inside, even from myself. I just wanted to make her
happy—to make her laugh. It was the most wonderful sound. It was
the first time I could remember that there was more to life than war."
He smiled sadly at the memory.

I wondered who *she* was. Who was the girl? Was it Dyana . . . or
someone else? I could not bring myself ask. I just let him go on. "I
heard the bird cry out. That's when we saw the trap. It was hanging
in a nearby tree. I should have told her to climb down, but I didn't. I
thought she was strong enough to hang on. It would have taken only
a second to cut the bird loose with my knife. I never should have left
her, but I did. I climbed over to the white hawk and left her alone in
the tree." He shamefully buried his face again.

The story was tragic. Tears ran over my cheeks before I even knew
the end. It didn't matter. I could see it in his face, and hear it in

his voice—the despair, the remorse, the guilt. "I didn't even have a chance to free the bird. It all happened so fast. There was a scream, and then she hit the water. I jumped in after her, but it was too late. The river took her. By the time I found her, she was gone. Adalynn was dead." The last sentence he spoke hung between us. He looked at me with tormented eyes.

"Adalynn?" I asked, confused. "But, she didn't die. They found her alive." Before my brain had a chance to process it all, I jerked away from the soldier in a sudden realization. "Oh no! Adalynn!"

I jumped up in a panic, and took off running. "What is it, Emilie?" the young man called after. He caught up to me, and we ran down the riverbank toward Kingsgrove.

The King Cemetery came into view. Ruby was kneeling before Adalynn, who was lying beneath the willow tree. "Ada!" I called out and Ruby looked up.

"*Cherie*! You are alive!" A smile crossed her tearstained face, and then she saw the soldier. Her thunderstruck expression was a conflicted facade of emotions.

I dropped down to the grass next to Adalynn. "Is she . . .?" I could not bear to say the word. My heart was breaking.

Before Ruby could answer, Adalynn's eyes opened. She saw the young man. He took her hand and held it tightly in his own. Adalynn smiled. To my surprise, she parted her lips and tried to speak, but there was only silence. At that exact moment, something dawned on me.

Miraculously, the messenger bag was still strapped across my chest. I undid the buckle and pulled out the wet female poppet. Everyone's eyes were on me as I tore away the red cloth that bound its mouth and hands. We all stared at the little doll, and hoped a spell had finally been broken. Together, we turned back to Adalynn. We did not speak. We did not even breathe. We just sat there and waited with anticipation. Miss King looked at the soldier, and then slowly parted her lips again.

It was hardly a whisper, but we all rejoiced at the sound of her voice. For the first time in fifty years, Adalynn King spoke. Her hazel eyes met a matching pair. She looked fondly at the young man and said a name. "Miles?"

He pressed her hand over his heart and replied, "It's me Ada. I'm free."

"Miles . . . my brother," Ada whispered again and smiled with quivering lips.

Brother? The soldier was her brother? Miles' story was about *his sister*, Adalynn! She drowned, and he pulled her dead body from the river. But if she died that day, how was she alive for all those years to follow? The questions and answers were coming too quickly. There was no time to make sense of their tangled past.

"I'm so sorry, Ada." Miles was choked with pain as he spoke to his sister. "It was my fault you fell. I had to do something. It was the only way to bring you back. I didn't know it would turn out like this. I never should have trusted Dyana. And she made you hold onto the truth this entire time." Miles shook his head and gritted his teeth in anger. "While everyone else was made to forget, she made you suffer in silence. I'm so sorry."

Adalynn smiled weakly at her brother, and said in a quiet voice, "It was an accident. You shouldn't have sacrificed yourself."

As Miss King spoke, the pieces started to fit. Everything was finally making sense. Miles had taken Adalynn's body to the Eventide's cabin where Dyana then preformed the necromancy spell. I remembered the Latin mantra.

Concede mortem ad cubiculum, obscuro infinitum. Pueri spiritus redeat ad corpus.

Yield to the death chamber, the dark infinity. Child's spirit returns to the body.

The child was Adalynn and Miles was the sacrifice! But instead of killing him, Dyana found a way to hide him in the dark, between the veils of life and death. She knew that if he died, he would crossover and she would never have him. In death, she would be denied passage, because she was a witch. If she trapped him in the dark, they would be joined in purgatory forever. When Miles went to her with his young sister lying dead in his arms, Dyana saw an opportunity. It was her chance to be with the man she loved for an eternity.

"She's dying," Ruby whispered, so only I could hear. My heart dropped. I looked at the small librarian, pleading with my eyes. Cheeks stained with tears, Ruby hugged me briefly then stood up. She said she was going to get help. Before leaving us, she mouthed a silent, *It will be ok*, in my direction. Even though it hurt, I understood. Adalynn was supposed to die when she was ten years old. It was meant to be. Fate was tampered with, and a balance had to be restored. Miles was given back the life he was meant to live. That meant it was time for Adalynn's life to end.

My heart shattered with grief, and I started to cry. Adalynn turned to me. She lifted a feeble hand and softly stroked my matted hair. "Thank you, Emilie," she said in a hushed tone. The woman did not look afraid. She was at peace as the light faded from her hazel eyes.

Adalynn passed away.

Miles and I wept as we sat next to her lifeless body. I looked up to the night sky, in despair. The moon still smiled its crooked smile, and the stars still shone brilliantly above.

Suddenly, amidst all the heartache, we heard the carefree laughter of a little girl. The heavenly sound lilted happily throughout the cemetery. We looked up and saw a young spirit standing by the river's edge. The girl smiled sweetly, and her lucid image flickered in and out of sight. She wore a pretty summer dress, and her long bronze hair flowed beautifully down her back. The girl was lovely. She looked to be around ten years old. It was a young Adalynn King. She spoke in a small resonating voice. "Miles! Isn't it wonderful? We're free!" The girl spun around, and her skirt danced playfully at her knees. "I'm so happy!" she sang out. "Emilie made everything right again."

Miles gazed at me with affection and affirmed, "She's remarkable."
My cheeks flushed at the amorous remark.

I looked at the girl's spirit and painfully declared, "I'm going to miss you Ada. So much." Warm tears poured heavily down my face. Even though we'd known each other for only short time, she was my friend. A friend I would remember and cherish forever.

The young spirit smiled warmly at me, and then turned to Miles. "Goodbye, my brother. I love you." With that, Adalynn turned away and walked slowly into the river. Her spirit dissolved on the water's surface into a delicate wisp of iridescent vapor.

FREE

I stood by an open window and took a deep breath of fresh air. A light gust of wind blew the curtain softy around me. I felt the delicate fabric caress my skin. The sensation helped to soothe my conflicted spirit.

I squinted at the mid-day sun and looked down to the cemetery below. Staring back at me were seven graves. The newest one rested under the weeping branches of the willow tree. I remembered the words engraved onto the granite stone.

She soars on wings of white,
And sings the song of freedom.

Adalynn's life was a mysterious tale of deception with a bitter-sweet end. It was an existence meant to be short-lived. Her true destiny was stolen with good intentions; a twisted mess created by a brother's love for his little sister. Miles refused to accept the truth. Out of desperation, he chose to trust the untrustworthy. He put their lives in the hands of a love-scorned witch. It was all in vain, for a path had been set. Fate had proven to be stronger than any magic. The universe refused to bow down to the evils that grew in Willow Vale.

I turned away from the window and looked at the room that was, until recently, my own. The space had been cleaned out, as of late. The bed was made with fresh sheets, the dresser drawers were emptied, and the old washroom was spotless and smelled of lemons.

It was strange to think that I had moved in only a month before. It looked the same, but felt so different. My life had changed drastically since that day. The time to move on had come again. The servant's quarters were no longer meant for me.

A few items of mine remained on the desk in the corner. I started to gather the pencils and books that lay scattered across the surface. Amongst the pile was the antique album that I found a few weeks prior. I ran my finger over the white bird on the cover and smiled at its significance. I opened the book and found a name and date, written in ink. The faded script read, *Miles King, Born April 4th 1923.* The scrapbook was full of delicate photographs of a baby boy. There were no more blank spaces and missing pictures. Everything had been restored. In fact, change had come to the entire house. All the empty frames, that hung on walls and sat on shelves, held pictures once more. Everything from childhood images of a boy to a young man in uniform appeared throughout the home. Those who had been forgotten were remembered once again. Kingsgrove was not a cursed creature forged with secrets and mystery any longer. It was a home built on family pride and love.

I placed the book back on the desk then felt for the locket at my neck. It was a gesture of habit. Sadly, my hand found nothing. The memento was still lost somewhere deep in the forest. My heart ached and my mind wandered back to an even greater loss.

A week had passed since the great room at Kingsgrove was teeming with the citizens of Willow Vale. Both the young and old came to say goodbye to Miss Adalynn King. Even the members of the Willow Vale Social Committee made an appearance. They huddled together and whispered about Kingsgrove and its preserved splendor. I tried my best to ignore it, but overheard them anyway.

"It's quite lush, but a bit gloomy, don't you think?" one woman said to another. "It's like we just stepped back in time." The group prattled on. "It looks positively haunted."

If only they knew.

Some people came, only to gawk at the aging estate, while others claimed to be friends of Ada's older sisters. They manhandled every photo album, and hemmed and hawed over the family's sophisticated beauty. I watched and listened carefully as one came across a photo of Miles. It was a candid snapshot of himself as a teenager. He was sitting on the front veranda, laughing at some long-forgotten joke.

"This must be the oldest son," a woman said to her friend. "I believe he went off to war and returned when it ended. But it was only for a short time, I reckon."

It was astounding how Dyana's spell had erased a person from existence. He had vanished from everything, even from memory. To be taken away and completely forgotten would be unfathomable. No words could describe the agony Adalynn must have felt. She knew everything, and lived with the truth sealed inside. The witch's curse trapped the memory of Miles inside Adalynn's mind for decades. Had she doubted her own sanity throughout the years? Over time, did she wonder if her brother was even real? Was he a delusion, or maybe just a dream?

Once Adalynn realized that I could see Miles, did it bring her hope?

Did she believe in herself again?

"It's a shame that there's no one to inherit the home. How strange, that there weren't any children or grandchildren," a rickety old woman said. The dusty feather on her hat quivered as she shook.

"Violet and Alice King couldn't have children," another woman gossiped. "And the twins never tried, as far as I recall. Tabitha Rose once told me that she couldn't bear to feel the disappointment. It's too bad. They would have made such pretty babies."

Scarlet Eventide made it very clear that she wanted Kingsgrove once Adalynn was dead and gone. Again, I wondered if the witches were behind the suspicious family condition, ensuring that the King sisters were not able to have children. The Eventides did everything in their power to please their selfish desires. It was scary to think how dangerously close they were to succeeding. Fortunately, despite all the elaborate spells and manipulations, they failed miserably in the end.

"Well hello there, young man." JoJo went to greet the newest visitor. "Thank you for coming. I'm Miss Peters. I was a dear friend of Adalynn's."

"Hello, Miss Peters." The handsome stranger smiled, and kissed the back of JoJo's hand.

The nurse tilted her head slightly in consideration. "Hey now. You look familiar." JoJo stepped back to look him up and down.

"Perhaps I should introduce myself," the young man spoke politely. "I am named after my late grandfather, Miles King, Adalynn's brother."

Miss Peters was clearly taken aback. I had slowly made my approach, and was standing next to her. The woman clutched a handful of her ruffled blouse, grabbed my arm to steady herself, and gasped. "Do you know what this means?" JoJo rejoiced in a breathless whisper.

"What's going on?" I asked.

"Oh Emilie, it is the most wonderful thing." She was shaking with excitement.

"What?" I smiled, acting bewildered.

JoJo crossed the room and snatched a photograph from the fireplace mantel. She held it at arm's length as she rushed back over to the young man. "Look, Emilie!" Miss Peters had my favorite photograph of Miles in her hand. It was a portrait of a soldier, colored in tones of grey and framed in brass. She held it up to his face and rejoiced. "It's incredible! He looks identical! Doesn't he, Emilie?"

"Yes. It looks like the same person." Miles and I shared a smile that possessed an untold secret.

"What is your name?" he asked me in front of JoJo.

"Emilie Wyld. I was Miss King's companion and caretaker," I replied.

"It's a pleasure to meet you." His lips lingered on the back of my hand. Delicious tingles rained over my entire body.

"Come with me. Both of you." Miss Peters gave the urgent command in a hushed voice.

People were listening. People would talk.

JoJo took Miles and me into the east parlor and closed the heavy doors behind us. I had not stepped foot in there since Ada had died. It was her favorite room in the estate. Seeing the wall of books, the old record player, and the half-knitted shawl hanging over the love-seat, twisted my stomach in heartache.

"Do you know what this means?" JoJo could hardly contain herself. "Kingsgrove is not for sale!"

"I'm sorry?" Miles did his best to sound confused.

"Adalynn made me executor of the will, you understand? Since she couldn't tell anyone what she wanted, she trusted me to do it for her. I'm too old to take care of this place by myself, so I was going to sell everything. It breaks my heart to think of such a thing. The truth is, this house belongs to a King. And here I thought there were none of you left." JoJo embraced Miles out of delight. "Is there anyone else besides you Miles?"

"Unfortunately, I was an only child and my parents died in an accident a few years ago. I'm the only one," Miles said everything exactly as we planned. Even I would have believed him, if I did not know the truth. "I heard about my great aunt's passing, so I came to pay my respects. I'm just sorry I didn't get meet her before."

"My goodness! I'm so sorry for all your loss!" JoJo held a hand over her mouth in distress. "Ada would have loved to meet you. You are the spittin' image of her brother. You are certainly a King. I can see it in those eyes. Can you see it, Emilie?"

I studied his face carefully. There was a hidden smile in the corner of his mouth. My cheeks burned. He had the ability to make me blush with just a simple look. "There is no doubt," I said with sincerity.

"That does it! I'll make all the arrangements. The house is yours if you want it Mr. King." The nurse waited anxiously for an answer.

"All right. I'll take it," he said with an unexpected joy. "But, only if Miss Wyld can stay and help me take care of it."

"Of course," I said without hesitation. "Kingsgrove is my home."

JoJo Peters clapped her hands together in jubilation. "Well now, I'm in seventh heaven. This is just perfection. I'll get a hold of the lawyer straight away." With that, she scampered off and left Miles and I alone in the parlor.

The second the coast was clear, we jumped into each other's arms. It had been a few days since we were together. With the chaos of planning the funeral, Miles was forced to stay away. He had spent the time with Ruby Monrose. She helped him update a few things. As it turns out, coming back to life after fifty years can be pretty complicated. Thankfully, the little librarian had proven to be quite resourceful. After pulling a few strings, and calling in a few favors, Miles had all the certificates and documents he needed to ease the transition into society.

"We did it, Emilie." He held me tight. His voice was full of relief. Kingsgrove was safe!

✗ ✗ ✗

My mind spun with all that took place after the funeral. The days had flown by, and so many things had changed. To clear my mind, I went back to cleaning the old servant's quarters. I gathered the last of my belongings and went into the hallway. My bare feet pattered on the hardwood floor through the empty estate. I came to a door hidden in the shadows of a small corridor. I turned the brass knob and pushed it open. The hinges creaked loudly in protest. Before me was a large bedroom, shrouded in darkness. The heavy curtains were drawn. I put my things down and walked across the floor. With both hands, I tore open the drapes and lifted the windowpane. The fresh, summer day poured in, and the space filled with sunlight. I looked around, smiled, and breathed a sigh of contentment.

The room was large and adorned. The cobwebs were swept away and the air was fragrant and sweet. A crisp, white duvet sat like a cloud atop the four-poster bed. Freshly picked magnolias were in a vase on the dresser, and a gallery of my artwork peppered the wall.

After my grandmother died, I felt lost. That lonely feeling was *finally* gone. I would never be cast aside or displaced ever again. Miles wanted us to be together. Kingsgrove was where we would stay, though I would follow him to the ends of the earth. With Miles, I was home at last.

A resounding chime rang through the upper floor of the estate. A grandfather clock struck three. I could not help but grin with excitement. It was time to go.

I left the bedroom and pranced through the long hallways of the west wing. My summer dress billowed as I cascaded down the grand staircase, slipped my sandals on, and dashed out the front door. A vintage Shwinn bicycle was resting against the front veranda. I hopped on and peddled down the long driveway. My hair lifted up and the blonde tresses blew in the wind. Never had I felt so free.

Butterflies tickled my stomach in anticipation as I rode the furrows and dips of Kings Lane. Miles had gone into town to take care of a few errands. I was supposed to meet him halfway, upon his return. Even though he was only gone a short while, I missed him all the same.

The site of our rendezvous was near. I peddled slowly until the wooded path was revealed. An old bicycle rested against the trunk of a tree in the aperture. *Willowmere Lake* was carved into a sun-bleached sign above. I laid my bike beside the other, and took to the trail by foot. The ground was cracked and dry from the baking sun. Tangled garlands of Spanish moss swayed from the arc of overhead branches. I lifted my arms to feel the matted veil sweep gently over them. It was my favorite place on earth. I cherished every sight, scent, and sound.

The trickle of rippling water made my heart skip a beat. The trail ended, and the shimmering lake appeared. I climbed onto a large root that was deeply anchored to the forest floor. I leaned against the ancient tree and admired the view. Miles stood at the edge of the dock. His silhouette was still as he looked out at the water. The surface was alive with fragmented daylight. That moment was mine to keep. A moment forever etched in memory to evoke at my desire.

I quietly removed my sandals and stepped out of the forest. I lifted my dress over my head and let it fall silently to the dock. The sun heated my exposed skin. Without a noise, I closed the space between us and just barely rested my chest to his back. The soft fabric of his cotton shirt brushed lightly against me. My hands travelled up his arms with the slightest touch. His breath hitched, and his muscles tightened in response. My own breathing turned heavy with desire.

Miles faced me and buried me in his arms. We kissed. His lips were starved, but gentle. In time, he pulled away. With his head bowed, his eyes looked up to mine. The hazel stare was eager and full of want. I found the hem of his shirt and raised it up. In one swift motion, he tore it off and tossed it aside. Miles grazed the back of his hand down my freckled arm. His hand met mine, and our fingers interlaced. Standing together, we turned toward Willowmere Lake. Our toes gripped the edge. We filled our lungs with air, bent our knees, and sprung from the dock.

Together, we vanished beneath the surface. The cool water consumed me as I fell deep into the dark basin. Once the descent slowed, I swam to the rippling light. I emerged and relished in the exhilaration. Miles came over, and we swam toward shallow water.

We waded in silence for a moment until our eyes met. I immediately noticed his sombre expression. Something troubled him.

"What's a matter?" I asked.

Miles reached out and pulled me close. The droplets on his face shone like crystals in the sun. "Emilie, there is something you need to know." The anxiety in his voice made my stomach twist. "Never in my wildest dreams could I have predicted you. A tenacious angel, sent to rescue me." He spoke with a soft intensity. His eyes were locked with mine. "I was awestruck the moment you walked into Kingsgrove. The darkness was set ablaze at the moment of your arrival. You drew me out with your radiant light, like a moth to a flame. All I could see was you. All I *still* see is you. You have stolen my heart and given me life. Love is only a word. A word could not describe the way I feel." It was more than a declaration. Something was left unsaid.

"Miles, don't you see? It was *you* who saved *me*. Before this, my life was empty . . . and disappointing. If I hadn't come to Kingsgrove, I would've been haunted my entire life. I didn't even know what I was missing, until I found it in you. If not for you, I would have been lost forever." He wrapped his arms around me and rested his head against mine.

"Scarlet's returned. I saw her open the emporium this afternoon." The mention of her name gave me a horrible chill. After Scarlet pushed me into the river, Ruby saw her break down. She realized her powers were stripped away then went into hysterics. The disarmed witch cursed us all before running off into the woods. Neither Scarlet nor Dyana had been seen or heard from since. We all wondered how long it would last. To be safe, Ruby preformed a cleansing on Kingsgrove after the funeral. Once the ritual was complete, the estate was transformed. It felt lighter and safe. The spicy scent of sage still lingered in the halls.

"The Eventide's are resentful and ruthless. Scarlett will have a personal vendetta against you. If her powers return, you'll never be safe," Miles said, and then held me at arm's length. "If she lays her hands on you again, I will kill her myself," he declared.

"Miles, I'm not afraid of Scarlet. I've never felt so safe in all my life." I tried to reassure him with a confident smile. "After all, do I not have a soldier at my side?"

"Air Force captain," Miles corrected me, trying to be serious and failing. A hidden smile shined in his hazel eyes.

"My apologies, Captain." I beamed.

With some playful persuasion, Miles began to relax. He took my face in his hands, kissed me briefly, and then dove into the water. Together, we swam to the middle of the lake. I twisted my body around to lie on my back. The sun blinded my eyes and the water deafened my ears. I floated effortlessly and carelessly along the fluid surface. My spirit was appeased.

Then a bird cried out.

The abrasive cawing was faint and stifled by the lapping water. I paid it no attention, until the sky suddenly went dark. It was a deviant eclipse of the sun. The light of day was obscured by a living omen. I stared up at the black beast, the shadow in flight—the raven in the sky.

ABOUT THE AUTHOR

As a child, Christena Rose loved her grandmother's ghost stories, even when she lost sleep over them for weeks. Now, she still loves a good ghost story, with a twist, and hopes to write the books she would love to read. Christena has a degree in graphic design and enjoys writing, reading, and art. Twisted Veil is her first book. She lives with her husband-to-be, daughter, dog, and cat.

CPSIA information can be obtained
at www.ICGtesting.com
Printed in the USA
BVHW031106070820
585651BV00002B/99

9 781525 539480